Kelly Andrews Refused To Fall Under Ryan Blackstone's Sensual Spell.

Going out on a date with him was out of the question. So carefully, with what she hoped was a conciliatory smile, Kelly responded to Ryan's request. "I'm flattered, but I'm afraid I'll have to decline your invitation. First of all, I'm tired—"

"And...?" he asked.

"And, second, I have a rule. *Don't date the boss!*"

To Kelly's surprise, Ryan started laughing.

"What's so funny?" she asked.

"You are," he said, sobering. "Since technically I'm not your boss, I guess you'll have to find another reason to reject my offer."

Bracing one hand on the door, Kelly smiled grimly. "Oh, really, well that'll be easy." Without warning she closed and locked the door in his face. "Good night, Ryan."

Ryan stood motionless. She'd actually slammed the door in his face. "Well, I'll be...."

Dear Reader,

Welcome to Silhouette Desire and another month of sensual tales. Our compelling continuity DYNASTIES: THE DANFORTHS continues with the story of a lovely Danforth daughter whose well-being is threatened and the hot U.S. Navy SEAL assigned to protect her. Maureen Child's *Man Beneath the Uniform* gives new meaning to the term *sleepover!*

Other series this month include TEXAS CATTLEMAN'S CLUB: THE STOLEN BABY with Cindy Gerard's fabulous *Breathless for the Bachelor*. Seems this member of the Lone Star state's most exclusive club has it bad for his best friend's sister. Lucky lady! And Rochelle Alers launches a brand-new series, THE BLACKSTONES OF VIRGINIA, with *The Long Hot Summer,* which is set amid the fascinating world of horse-breeding.

Anne Marie Winston singes the pages with her steamy almost-marriage-of-convenience story, *The Marriage Ultimatum*. And in *Cherokee Stranger* by Sheri WhiteFeather, a man gets a second chance with a woman who wants him for her first time. Finally, welcome brand-new author Michelle Celmer with *Playing by the Baby Rules,* the story of a woman desperate for a baby and the hunky man who steps up to give her exactly what she wants.

Here's hoping Silhouette Desire delivers exactly what *you* desire in a powerful, passionate and provocative read!

Best,

Melissa Jeglinski

Melissa Jeglinski
Senior Editor, Silhouette Desire

Please address questions and book requests to:
Silhouette Reader Service
U.S.: 3010 Walden Ave., P.O. Box 1325, Buffalo, NY 14269
Canadian: P.O. Box 609, Fort Erie, Ont. L2A 5X3

The Long Hot Summer

ROCHELLE ALERS

Published by Silhouette Books
America's Publisher of Contemporary Romance

SILHOUETTE BOOKS

ISBN 0-373-76565-7

THE LONG HOT SUMMER

Copyright © 2004 by Rochelle Alers

All rights reserved. Except for use in any review, the reproduction
or utilization of this work in whole or in part in any form by any
electronic, mechanical or other means, now known or hereafter
invented, including xerography, photocopying and recording, or in
any information storage or retrieval system, is forbidden without
the written permission of the editorial office, Silhouette Books,
233 Broadway, New York, NY 10279 U.S.A.

All characters in this book have no existence outside the imagination of
the author and have no relation whatsoever to anyone bearing the same
name or names. They are not even distantly inspired by any individual
known or unknown to the author, and all incidents are pure invention.

This edition published by arrangement with Harlequin Books S.A.

® and TM are trademarks of Harlequin Books S.A., used under license.
Trademarks indicated with ® are registered in the United States Patent
and Trademark Office, the Canadian Trade Marks Office and in other
countries.

Visit Silhouette at www.eHarlequin.com

Printed in U.S.A.

Books by Rochelle Alers

Silhouette Desire

A Younger Man #1479
*The Long Hot Summer #1565

*The Blackstones of Virginia

ROCHELLE ALERS

is a native New Yorker who lives on Long Island. She admits to being a hopeless romantic, who is in love with life. Rochelle's hobbies include traveling, music, art and preparing gourmet dinners for friends and family members. A cofounder of Women Writers of Color, Rochelle was the first proud recipient of the Vivian Stephens Career Achievement Award for Excellence in Romance Novel Writing. You can contact her at P.O. Box 690, Freeport, NY 11520-0690, or roclers@aol.com.

Dedicated to Isaac Murphy—the first jockey of any race to win the Kentucky Derby three times.

Sons, listen to what your father teaches you.
Pay attention, and you will have understanding.
—*Proverbs* 4:1

One

"**W**ho the hell are you?"

Startled by the voice below where she stood on a stepladder hanging a colorful border of zoo animals above a corkboard—a booming voice sounding as if it had come from the bowels of the earth—Kelly Andrews lost her balance and fell backward. Her fall was halted as she found herself cushioned against the solid chest of the man who had silently entered the schoolhouse.

A swooshing rush of breath escaped her parted lips at the same time her eyes widened in surprise. Glaring down at her under lowered lids was the man who was her tormentor and rescuer.

There was no doubt he was a Blackstone. The angular, raw-boned face was the same as Sheldon Blackstone's. His eyes were gray, not the silvery sparkling shade of his father's, but a dark gray that reminded Kelly of a wintry sky before a snowstorm.

She wondered which Blackstone son he was— Jeremy the DEA agent or Ryan the veterinarian. Whoever he was, the black stubble on his jaw made him look formidable. Her startled gaze settled on his sensual full lower lip, wondering if it ever softened in a spontaneous smile.

Ryan Blackstone's expression mirrored that of the woman in his arms: shock. He'd just returned to Virginia and Blackstone Farms from the Tuskegee University of Veterinary Medicine where he'd taught several courses as a visiting professor for two semesters.

Minutes after he'd parked his car in the garage near the main house he had noted the sly grins and muted whispers from long-time employees, but chose to ignore them because he had been anxious to reunite with his father. His four-year-old son had spent the drive from Alabama to Virginia chattering incessantly about returning to the horse farm and seeing Grandpa.

Sheldon had warmly welcomed his son and grandson home, then told Ryan that he wanted him to meet the teacher for the new child care center, at the same time extolling the woman's credentials and experience. This news pleased Ryan because now the young children who lived at Blackstone Farms would have a structured daily environment. For years they had become free spirits, wood sprites with the horse farm's property as their backyard. They ran barefoot in the grass, climbed trees, swam in one of the two in-ground pools and raced in and out of the dining hall several times a day for snacks. Establishing the Blackstone Day School was an ideal situation, but only if the woman in his arms wasn't its new teacher.

Kelly placed a palm on his chest, pushing against solid muscle. "Please, put me down, Mr. Blackstone."

The sound of her husky voice jolted Ryan. The soft, perfumed body pressed against his was so pleasurable that he'd almost forgotten how good it felt to hold a woman—especially one who was certain *not* to share his bed.

Dark gray eyes narrowed slightly under raven eyebrows. He held his breath before letting it out slowly. "Who's asking?" He had tightened his grip under her knees.

"Kelly Andrews, Blackstone Farms Day School's new teacher. And I hope you don't make it a habit of using profanity around children."

Ryan glared at Kelly. Who did she think she was? "What did you say?"

"Mr. Blackstone, if you're hearing impaired I can sign for you. I'm certified in American Sign Language as well as certified to teach nursery through sixth grade. Now, I'm going to ask you again to put me down or I'll be forced to show you what other certifications I have."

Ryan decided he liked holding Kelly. He liked the husky timbre of her voice and the way her curvy body melded with his; he also liked the smell of her hair and skin.

"Are you warning me that you're trained in martial arts?"

Smiling, Kelly admired the masculine face inches from her own. Slanting cheekbones, a strong nose with slightly flaring nostrils, and a square-cut chin made for an arresting visage. His eyes were beautiful. They were a striking contrast to his brown skin.

Slowly, as if in a trance, Ryan lowered Kelly until her sandaled feet touched the newly installed oak flooring.

So, he thought, she *was* the one everyone had been whispering about. She was the teacher who would assume the responsibility for socializing the farm's young children. Studying her upturned face, Ryan stared down into eyes the color of newly minted pennies with glints of gold. They were framed by long, thick black lashes, which seemed to enhance their vibrancy. Her delicate copper-brown face was exquisite: sculpted cheekbones and a delicate chin with a hint of a dimple. A slight smile tugged at the corners of his mouth. Kelly Andrews was lovely; no, he mused, she was stunning!

When Ryan had walked into the schoolhouse, he'd stood there mutely, staring at a pair of incredibly long legs under a pair of cutoffs, a narrow waist and slim hips. The hem of her sleeveless white blouse was tied at her midriff, offering a glimpse of velvety flesh at a waist small enough for him to span with both hands. Her dark chemically relaxed hair, cut to graze the back of her long neck, was secured off her face by a wide red headband.

"How old are you, Miss Andrews?"

Kelly took a quick breath of utter astonishment. Counting slowly to herself, she bit down on her lower lip. She had to choose her words wisely or she would walk away from this position.

Staring up at the tall man looming over her, she forced a smile she did not feel. "In case you aren't aware of it, Mr. Blackstone, but there are laws against age discrimination in the workplace." A spark of satisfaction lit her eyes when a rush of deep color darkened his tanned gold-brown face.

Ryan's right hand tightened at his side. "I'm very much aware of the law, Miss Andrews," he said. "And you can call me Ryan. My father is Mr. Blackstone."

Even though Sheldon Blackstone was legally

listed as owner of the horse farm, it was Ryan who had eventually assumed responsibility for its day-to-day operation. His father had resumed the role this past year only because Ryan had been teaching as a visiting professor at his alma mater. In Ryan's absence Sheldon had advertised, interviewed and had hired Kelly to teach the children of Blackstone Farms.

And given Sheldon's penchant for beautiful women, it was obvious why he had hired Kelly An-drews.

Pulling herself up to her full five-foot-eight-inch height, Kelly flashed a confident grin. ''If you're that versed in the law, then why did you inquire about my age?''

Aware that he'd been caught in a trap of his own making, Ryan struggled to extricate himself from a terminal case of foot-in-mouth.

''You look so young that I...I,'' he stammered, unable to complete his statement. There was something in her gaze that tightened the muscles in his stomach. It had been a long time since a woman had excited him with just a glance. Not since the first time his gaze met the woman's who had eventually become his wife and the mother of his son.

Kelly lifted an eyebrow and decided to let Ryan squirm a bit longer. It would serve him right if she turned her back on him and went back to decorating her classroom. She had wanted to finish by the end of what had become a very long day.

But there was so much to do. She still had to unpack and catalog books, games, art supplies and videos before she'd be ready. She had hoped to open the school on Monday—exactly one month since her arrival at Blackstone Farms.

"I can assure you, *Ryan,*" she said, stressing his name, "I'm old enough *and* qualified to teach."

"That may be so, Miss Andrews, but I intend to monitor you closely during your probationary period."

Gazing up at him, Kelly noticed a sprinkling of silver in the thick, close-cropped wavy black hair. There was something rakish and sophisticated in Ryan. His dark skin and light colored eyes reminded her of lightning in a bottle.

"Ryan?" Her voice was soft and layered with a sensuality that jerked his head up like a marionette manipulated by a puppeteer.

His eyes darkened until they were nearly black with an indefinable emotion. "Yes, Kelly." It was the first time he'd called her by her given name.

Tilting her chin, she gave him a captivating smile. "I don't have a probationary clause in my contract."

Ryan closed his eyes, silently cursing his father for being taken in by her pretty face. It was Sheldon who had vehemently insisted that everyone employed at Blackstone Farms sign a contract—one that always included a clause detailing a probationary period.

He opened his eyes to find Kelly staring at him, while at the same time the curvy pout of her sexy mouth taunted and challenged him. "What did you promise my father?"

Her smooth forehead furrowed. "Excuse me?"

Ryan leaned closer. "You heard me the first time, Kelly. Don't make me have to sign for *you*." His gaze roamed leisurely over her body. "I hope when you begin teaching you'll be wearing more clothes."

Without giving her an opportunity to come back at him, he turned on his heels, walked out of the schoolhouse, and closed the door softly, leaving her to stare at a pair of broad shoulders that seemed almost too wide for the doorway.

She sat on the stepladder, her shoulders slumping in resignation as the enthusiasm she had felt earlier that morning dissipated. It did not take the intelligence of a rocket scientist to know that Ryan Blackstone did not like women. And apparently it wasn't all women—just the younger ones.

At thirty, she had experienced what most women her age hadn't: widowhood. Several months before she'd celebrated her twenty-eighth birthday Simeon Randall had been killed by a hit-and-run driver when he'd pulled off the parkway to fix a flat tire.

Simeon, mercifully, had died instantly from massive head trauma.

The appearance of two police officers at her door, asking that she come to a local hospital because her husband had been killed in a traffic accident had changed her and her life forever. She'd lost her first love, soul mate and life partner. Even after she had buried her husband she refused to accept that he would not walk through the door each night to share dinner with her. She'd continued to set the table for two. When her mother, who had come to see her without calling first, asked about the extra place setting, Kelly broke down and sobbed in her arms the way she'd done as a child. Camille Andrews stayed the night, holding her daughter in her arms while they slept in the bed Kelly had shared with her son-in-law.

The following day Kelly walked into the principal's office at the school where she'd taught third grade, and resigned her position. Two days later she got into her car and headed for Washington, D.C. to spend time with her sister and brother-in-law. A month's stay became two, and eventually twenty-three.

She had returned to New York City to clean out her co-op apartment, sell items she did not want, place heirloom pieces in storage and list the property with a real estate agent. The apartment was sold six months later, and Kelly deposited the pro-

ceeds into a Washington, D.C., bank account. She
continued to pay to store her furniture until she received official documentation of her hire as a
teacher for Blackstone Farms Day School. The antique mahogany sleigh bed, armoire, heirloom lin-
ens, quilts and the wrought-iron table and chairs
that had once sat on her grandmother's patio now
graced the charming bungalow she would call home
for the next year.

She sat on the stool until the door opened again,
and this time it was Sheldon Blackstone who had
come to see her. "Don't bother to get up," he said,
as he came closer. Leaning against the wall, he
crossed his legs at the ankles. "It looks nice, Miss
Kelly."

She nodded. "I should finish decorating tonight."

A slight frown marred Sheldon's lined forehead.
"Why don't you put that off until tomorrow?"

Kelly studied the older man's profile, finding him
quite handsome. Tall, solidly built, with brilliant
light-gray eyes in a face the color of toasted pecans,
she knew the widowed horse breeder could easily
attract a woman from thirty to eighty.

"Why?"

"Everyone's gathering in the dining hall tonight
at six to welcome my son and grandson home."
Since coming to Blackstone Farms Sheldon noticed

that Kelly rarely took her meals in the dining hall with the other employees.

She nodded. "I'll be there, Mr. Blackstone."

Straightening, he wagged a finger at her. "I told you before that we're pretty informal here. Please call me Sheldon."

"If that's the case, please call me Kelly."

"No," he said, shaking his head. "I'll call you *Miss* Kelly in front of the children. There's an unwritten rule here. The children aren't allowed to address adults by their given name, especially women. I know it may sound outdated and quite Southern to a Northerner, but it is a Blackstone tradition."

Kelly smiled. "I may be from New York, but I do claim some Southern roots. I have some Virginia blood on my daddy's side and South Carolina on my mama's."

Sheldon flashed a rare smile. "Where in Virginia?"

"Newport News."

"The best seafood I've ever eaten was in Newport News."

"I have relatives there who are fishermen."

Sheldon took a quick glance at his watch. "I expect to see you later."

"You will."

Kelly had to smile. *I expect to see you later.* It was Sheldon's way of ordering her to eat with the other employees. Since she had come to live on the farm, she had eaten at the dining hall twice, both times for breakfast. Sheldon had informed her that breakfast and lunch were served buffet-style, while dinner was a sit-down affair where everyone who lived or worked on the property shared in this meal—all except for her.

She usually prepared a light dinner, cleaned up the kitchen in the bungalow before throwing all of her energies into her craft projects. She'd worked practically nonstop to ready her classroom for the projected first day of school, which was now only three days away.

Curbing the urge to salute her boss, she watched as he walked across the floor of the spacious out-building that had been converted into a schoolhouse. She wanted to say *like father, like son,* but decided to reserve judgment on the Blackstones. After all, they were responsible for an enterprise that included thousands of acres of land, millions of dollars in horseflesh and a payroll for more than thirty employees.

After seeing an ad in *The Washington Post* for an experienced teacher certified in early childhood education to teach on a horse farm in the western part of Virginia, Kelly had searched the Internet for information on Blackstone Farms. She had learned that Blackstone Farms was one of a few owned and operated African American horse farms in the state.

She liked this part of Virginia. It was so different from New York City and Washington, D.C. Although it was early summer, the heat and humidity were noticeably lower. The property, west of the Blue Ridge and east of the Shenandoah Mountain ranges, lay in a valley like a shimmering emerald on blue-black velvet, was to become her home for the next year.

She glanced at her watch. It was almost four-thirty. She would finish putting up the banner, then go home to prepare for dinner.

Twenty minutes later, the border in place, Kelly walked out of the schoolhouse, closing the door behind her. Sheldon had introduced her to some of the other employees, but tonight would be the first time she would interact with all of them socially. It would also be the first time she would meet the parents of the children who would become her responsibility.

Attending the dinner would also bring her face-to-face with Ryan Blackstone again. He'd caught her off guard when he'd entered the schoolhouse undetected, but she made a solemn promise it would be the last time he would catch her off guard.

Two

Kelly parked her Honda between two late-model pickup trucks and stepped out into an area set aside for parking. It was fifteen minutes before six, yet the lot was almost filled to capacity. She hadn't taken more than a few steps when she saw him.

Ryan was dressed in black: linen shirt, slacks and low-heeled boots. The color made him appear taller, more imposing. Although he'd slowed his stride to accommodate the pace of the young child clinging to his hand, Kelly still admired the fluidity of his beautifully proportioned physique. There was something about Ryan that reminded her of her Simeon even though the two men looked nothing alike.

"It's a beautiful evening, isn't it, Miss Kelly?" Cooling mountain breezes ruffled the leaves of trees, bringing with it the cloying sweetness of wildflowers blooming throughout the valley.

Kelly stopped in midstride, her breathing halting momentarily before starting up again. Ryan had also stopped and turned around to face her. He stood several feet away, flashing a wide, white-tooth smile.

Recovering quickly, she returned his smile. "Yes, it is, Dr. Blackstone." Her gaze shifted to the boy staring up at her. Kelly knew the child was a Blackstone. He had inherited his father's features. His eyes were a mirror image of Ryan's. She extended her hand. She knew from the records Sheldon had given her that Sean Blackstone had recently celebrated his fourth birthday.

Bending at the knees, she said, "Hi."

Ryan placed a hand on his son's head. "Sean, this is Miss Kelly. She's going to be your teacher. Miss Kelly, this is my son, Sean."

Sean stared at her hand and inched closer to his father's leg. Vertical lines appeared between his large eyes. "I don't want to go to school."

Ryan hadn't registered his son's protest because all of his attention was directed at the woman dressed in a sheer white silk blouse, slim black linen wrap skirt and black heels.

He hadn't known Kelly was behind him until

he'd detected the scent of her perfume. Her exposed arms and legs shimmered with a dewy glow from a scented cream that sent a jolt of electricity through his body. Biting down on his lower lip, he struggled for control.

Sean tugged at his father's hand. "Do I have to go to school, Daddy?"

"Yes, you do."

Sean pushed out his lower lip. "But I don't want to."

"We've talked about his, Sean." Ryan's voice held a thread of hardness.

"No! I'm not going. I hate school!"

Kelly stared at Sean for several seconds. It was apparent the child was as stubborn and opinionated as his father. "School's not so bad," Kelly said, trying to calm the little boy down. "How about coming by the schoolhouse after dinner to check it out?"

Tears filled the boy's eyes. "No!"

Ryan opened his mouth to reprimand his son for being rude, but Kelly shook her head. Threatening or bullying the child was not the solution. She'd discovered gentle persuasion usually worked well with young ones.

She met Ryan's gaze. "I'm going to hold an open house for all of the children tomorrow morning at ten to show them their new school." She stared at Sean. "You are more than welcome to come."

She hadn't planned to show the children their new classroom until Monday morning, but she would make an exception if it meant winning Sean over.

Tightening his grip on Kelly's elbow, Ryan led her and Sean toward the entrance to the dining hall. Leaning closer, his moist breath sweeping over her ear, he whispered, "Thank you."

Holding the door open, Ryan permitted Kelly and Sean to precede him into a large, one-story brick building that had been referred to over the years as the dining hall. The entryway was crowded with people, some he had known for most of his life. The tantalizing aromas coming from the kitchen reminded him that he had come home.

He reached for Sean's hand while his free hand rested at the small of Kelly's back as if it were a gesture he'd done many times before. She stiffened slightly before relaxing her back beneath his splayed fingers.

Closing her eyes briefly, Kelly endured Ryan's touch and his closeness. It reminded her of what she had missed. There was never a time when she went out with Simeon that he hadn't silently announced she was his. Whether it was cradling her hand in the bend of his elbow, or circling her waist with an arm, he'd communicated possession and protection. She opened her eyes to find Ryan staring at her, his expression impassive.

"Have you met everyone?"

Kelly shook her head, thick dark strands moving fluidly with the slight motion.

"I haven't had the time," she explained in a soft voice. "It took me a week to settle into my bungalow, and all of my free time has been spent readying the classroom for Monday."

He frowned. "Why didn't you get someone to help you?"

"I did. Your father made Dennis available for me whenever I needed to move or lift something heavy."

Kelly, Sean and Ryan walked into the central dining hall amid a rousing round of applause and whistles. Sheldon stood under a colorful hand painted banner reading: Welcome To Blackstone Farms. Red and black helium-filled balloons—the colors of the farms' silks—tied with contrasting ribbons served as centerpieces for each white cloth-covered table. A dozen tables, each with seating for four, were filling up with employees who lived on the property.

Sheldon motioned Ryan closer. "You, Sean and Miss Kelly will sit with me."

Ryan pulled out a chair for Kelly, seating her while Sheldon performed the same motion for his grandson. He ruffled the child's curly black hair.

Kelly removed the strap to the tiny black purse she'd slung over her chest, placing the crocheted bag on her lap. Her gaze swept around the large room.

The exterior of the dining hall, as with most of the buildings on the farm, was deceiving. Simply constructed of brick or wood, the interior was extraordinary. The dining hall's furnishings rivaled those of any upscale restaurant in any major city. Dark paneled walls with decorative moldings, wide windows with stained-glass insets, plush carpeting, cloth-covered mahogany tables, Tiffany-style table lamps, fine china, crystal stemware, sterling silver and softly played taped classical selections set the stage for exquisite meals prepared by a resident chef.

Blackstone Farms was a thriving, profitable working horse farm and Sheldon had made certain it maintained a certain image given the numerous purses won by Blackstone champion Thoroughbreds over the years.

Still on his feet, Sheldon held a goblet filled with sparkling water. Raising a hand, he signaled for silence. "This isn't going to take long." A ripple of laughter followed his announcement.

"Yeah, right," Kevin Manning, the head trainer called out.

Sheldon put down his glass and crossed his arms over his chest, glaring at his lifelong friend. "You keep running off at the mouth and I'll pull out my prepared speech.''

''No!'' came a collected groan from everyone in the room.

Kelly glanced at Ryan when he threw back his head and laughed. Her gaze was fixed on his strong throat. So, she thought, he can laugh. The gesture changed his face, softening it.

Sheldon inclined his head. ''May I continue?''

''Please,'' Kevin said, raising a hand in supplication.

''Tonight is very special not only to me,'' Sheldon continued, ''but to everyone at Blackstone Farms. I get to have my son and grandson back for what I hope is more than a few months, and I want all of us to welcome the newest member of our farm family, Miss Kelly Andrews, the new teacher and director of Blackstone Farms Day School.''

All gazes were fixed on Kelly. She felt a wave of heat sweep up her chest and settle in her cheeks as everyone applauded. She was grateful for her darker coloring otherwise they would have been able to see the blush burning her face. She jumped noticeably when Ryan placed a hand over hers.

''You're expected to say a few words,'' he whispered, his mouth pressed to her ear. She jumped again, this time from the moist breath flowing into her ear. Rising, he pulled back her chair, assisting her as she stood up. He stood beside her, his left hand resting against her spine.

Composing herself, Kelly flashed a smile, eliciting gasps of appreciation from several men seated at a nearby table. "I'd like to thank Sheldon and everyone for their kindness and assistance in helping me set up the school." Her beautifully modulated husky voice was hypnotic. Her gaze swept around the room and settled on Sean. "I'm hosting an open house at the schoolhouse tomorrow morning at ten for everyone, especially the children, to give you an idea of what I've planned for the coming year. School begins officially Monday morning at eight o'clock, but for parents who want to drop their children off earlier, please let me know tomorrow." She smiled again. "Thank you."

Ryan seated Kelly, flashing a smile that signaled his approval. Listening to her speak, it was easy to tell she wasn't a Southerner. It was also obvious that she wasn't married, and in that instant he knew he wanted to know more about Miss Kelly Andrews. He knew he could go through her personnel file to glean her vital statistics, but it was the personal information he wanted. Did she have an ex-husband or a lover?

His musings were interrupted when a young woman approached the table to take their orders. Kelly studied the printout of the dinner choices. Appetizers included curried corn-crab cakes, sesame shrimp with a miso dipping sauce, and skewered spiced pork and red pepper with a spicy mango sauce. Entrées included grilled steak, broiled salmon, and roast chicken along with an assortment of steamed and grilled vegetables.

Leaning to her right, her breast brushed Ryan's shoulder and he turned and stared at her, the dark pupils in his eyes dilating. Their gazes caught and fused as their breathing found a common rhythm. Within a matter of seconds Kelly registered the overt virility Ryan exuded just by breathing. His warmth, the clean masculine scent of his body, the sensual fragrance of his cologne, and the penetrating gray eyes that appeared to see everything, miss nothing.

"What do you recommend?"

"Everything," he said in a soft voice as he continued to stare at her under lowered lids.

"How's the salmon?"

A slight frown marred his smooth forehead. "You've never eaten Cook's salmon?" Salmon had become a regular Friday night selection.

"I've never eaten dinner here."

His frown deepened. "Where have you been eating?"

"I cook for myself."

"Why would you cook for yourself when we have a resident chef?"

Kelly heard the censure in his question. "I've

been working long hours, and by the time I leave the schoolhouse the dining hall is closed.''

"You can always put in a request to have your dinner delivered to you."

She lifted a shoulder. "No one ever told me I could do that."

"Well, I'm telling you."

Kelly studied his grim expression, willing he smile again. Raising her dimpled chin slightly, a smile trembled over her full lips, drawing one from him. "Thank you for the information, Ryan." His name had become a whispered caress on her lips.

Sheldon sat across the table from his son and Kelly, watching a subtle game of seduction being played out in front of him. He doubted whether Ryan or Kelly were aware of their entrancement with the other.

Less than an hour ago he and Ryan had had a short and pointed discussion about his decision to hire Kelly Andrews. And it was the first time in years that he had used his status as majority owner in Blackstone Farms to counter Ryan's opinion. Ryan thought they should've hired a teacher with more experience. Sheldon had ended the conversation, stating that Ryan should find a woman to release his sexual frustration, and then walked out of the room leaving his firstborn with his mouth gaping.

It was never Sheldon's intent to become a match-maker, and he knew Ryan had never been involved with any woman who lived or worked at the farm. But, watching Kelly the past three weeks he suspected she would be able to handle herself when it came to his son just fine.

She had proven that once Dennis Poole had tried to come on to her when she'd asked him to move several boxes that had been delivered to the school-house. Dennis had confided to one of the grooms that Kelly told him that if he ever tried to touch her again she would change his gender in a New York minute. Dennis wasn't certain what she meant by the statement, but had decided it wasn't worth the risk to find out.

Sheldon gave his dinner selection to the waitress, thinking it would be nice to have another grand-child before he turned sixty. Ryan had made him a grandfather once already, but he looked forward to spoiling more than one of the next generation of Blackstones.

Kelly thoroughly enjoyed her dinner. The salmon was exquisite. The freshly caught fish, packed in ice the day before, had been flown from the North-west. Dinner conversation was light and entertain-ing as she listened to Sheldon and Ryan talk about horses while Sean politely interrupted his father several times to ask a question. Kelly found the boy quiet and somewhat withdrawn, and she wondered how much contact he'd had with his mother.

Two hours after dinner began, people began drifting over to the table to introduce themselves to Kelly and to welcome Ryan and Sean back home. Young children hid shyly behind their parents when Kelly told them she expected to see them the following morning at the schoolhouse.

Touching her napkin to the corners of her mouth, she pushed back her chair. Smiling at Ryan and Sheldon, she said, "Thank you, gentlemen, for your company. Dinner was wonderful." Both Blackstone men came to their feet, Ryan helping her to stand. She smiled at Sean, who wouldn't look at her. "I hope to see you tomorrow morning, Sean." Frowning, he pushed out his lower lip.

Sheldon winked at Kelly. "I'll take care of everything."

Picking up her crocheted purse, she opened it, and took out her keys. "Good evening."

Ryan reached for her hand, tucking it into the curve of his elbow. "I'll walk you to your car."

Her eyes widened. "That's all right. I believe I can find my way to the parking lot." There was a hint of laughter in her voice.

"I want to apologize to you."

"For what?"

He leaned closer. "I'll tell you later."

Sean rounded the table and tugged at Ryan's arm. "Daddy, can I stay with Grandpa tonight?"

Ryan glanced down at his son before looking at his father. Sheldon nodded. "Of course. You have to listen to Grandpa or it will be a long time before you'll be permitted to sleep over again. Do you understand?"

Sean flashed a wide smile, showing a mouth filled with tiny white teeth. "Yes, Daddy." Turning, he launched himself against Sheldon's body.

Ryan escorted Kelly to the parking lot. "My father will bring Sean to your open house tomorrow."

"Are you sure he'll be able to get him to come?"

"My father can get Sean to do anything. The child worships him because Sheldon spoils him."

Standing next to her car, Kelly smiled at Ryan in the waning daylight. "That's what grandparents are suppose to do—spoil their grandchildren."

He nodded, extending his hand. "Please give me your keys."

She tightened her grip. "Why?"

"I'll drive you back to your place."

"Don't be ridiculous, Ryan. I live less than a quarter of a mile from here."

Reaching for her hand, he gently pried her fingers apart. "I know where you live."

"But Ryan—"

"But nothing," he said softly, cutting her off.

"How will you get back?"

"I'll walk."

Opening the passenger-side door, he held it open for her. His gaze lingered on the expanse of her bare legs and feet in the high heels as her skirt shifted upward when she sat down. Rounding the car, he slipped in behind the wheel, adjusted the seat, and put the key in the ignition in one, smooth motion. The engine turned over and he backed out of the lot. Three minutes later he parked her compact sedan alongside Kelly's bungalow. The sun had set, leaving the sky with feathery streaks of orange crisscrossing a backdrop of navy-blue. Pinpoints of light from millions of twinkling stars emerged in the encroaching darkness.

Within minutes the landscape was completely black, except for an occasional light coming from windows in buildings spread out over the seventy-two hundred acres making up Blackstone Farms. The farm was laid out in a quadrangle: the main house, dining hall, and school in one quad; the barn, stables, paddocks and grazing area in the second; the cottages for resident employees in the third, and the last quadrant left for future expansion.

The farm was secure and protected by closed-circuit cameras strategically placed throughout the property, and at no time could anyone arrive or leave undetected.

Kelly waited for Ryan to come around and assist her. He opened the door and she placed her hand on his as he tightened his grip and pulled her gently to her feet. He was standing close, too close, but she did not attempt to pull away.

Holding out her hand, she said, "My keys, please."

Ignoring her request, he led her up the porch and to the door. He unlocked it, pushed it open, and then dropped the keys in her palm. The glow from a table lamp in the parlor spilled a ribbon of light out into the night.

"Thank you for seeing me to my door."

The sultry sound of Kelly's voice swept over Ryan like an invisible caress. "Thank you for a lovely evening. Sharing dinner with you helped make my homecoming even more special."

Kelly stared at the highly polished toes on Ryan's low-heeled boots rather than look into his eyes. "Good night."

Reaching out, his right hand cupped her chin, forcing her to meet his gaze. "I'm sorry."

"For what?" Her voice had dropped to a whisper.

"For using profanity, for being rude and for acting like a complete ass."

"Ryan!"

He flashed a wide grin. "I could've said ass…"

"No," she screamed, covering her ears with her hands.

Releasing her chin, he curved his arms around

her waist. "Don't tell me you're a prude, Miss Kelly."

She placed her hands over his chest. "I'm not a prude. It's just that I've heard enough profanity to last two lifetimes. You can't imagine the words I've heard from kids as young as five or six. A lot of them can't string a sentence together using the correct verb, yet they can cuss you out using words that can make the most jaded adult cringe."

Ryan lifted an eyebrow. "Whenever I cursed as a kid my mother used to wash my mouth out with lye soap. After awhile I learned never to curse in front of her. She refused to accept my rationale that if Pop said it, then it had to be all right."

"I hope you don't use those words around your son."

He shook his head. "Never."

"Good." She eased out of his loose embrace. "I have to go in now."

He did not want her to go in. He wanted to sit out under the stars and talk—talk about…

"Good night, Kelly."

She stared at him for several seconds. "Good night, Ryan."

Kelly stood on the porch, watching Ryan as he turned and walked away. Within minutes he disappeared and was swallowed up by the warm early summer night.

Three

Ryan walked back to his house, his mind filled with images of Kelly. During the evening meal he had watched her, admiring her natural beauty and the ease in which she seemed to accept her femininity.

She had sat upright, spine pressed against her chair, shoulders pulled back and her full breasts thrusting forward. He had felt like a voyeur whenever he watched her breasts rising and falling in an even rhythm. She had worn a lacy camisole under her blouse, and he had fantasized unbuttoning the blouse to run his fingertips over her skin.

Although he had been divorced for three years

he had not lived a monkish existence. The day he signed his divorce papers he'd driven to Waynesboro, gone to a local bar and drank himself into oblivion. He woke up hours later in a woman's bedroom with a hangover that had him retching for hours. It was the first and last time he had gotten drunk.

Once he cleansed his mind and body of the alcohol, he'd called his father to let him know he was still alive. He spent the next day baring his soul to a stranger. Lisa—she wouldn't tell him her last name—was eight years his senior, but she had become his confidante and eventually his lover. Their on-and-off-again relationship ended abruptly last Christmas when she called him to say him she had decided to remarry her ex-husband. He wished her well, and mailed her a generous check as a wedding gift.

In light of his casual attitude toward women, he simply couldn't understand the intensity of his initial attraction to Kelly. There was something so deeply alluring about her that he wanted to lie with her, damn the consequences.

He arrived at his house and opened the door. The moment he walked inside he felt the emptiness. Whenever Sean spent the night with Sheldon or overnight with one of his little pals, the emptiness was magnified. He thought he would get used to the loneliness, but it never seemed to dissipate completely.

It had begun several months after he'd married Caroline Harding, a young woman he'd met in college. She had begun to withdraw from him the day she found out she was pregnant. As her pregnancy progressed she confessed to feeling trapped, that she hated living on the farm, and pleaded with Ryan to let her out of their marriage. He'd granted her wish, and she got into her car, drove away from Blackstone Farms two months after she had given birth to a baby boy—alone.

Climbing the staircase to the second story, he walked into his bedroom and prepared to go to bed—alone.

Even though Kelly had been in bed for eight hours, she woke up fatigued. She'd spent the night dreaming and tossing restlessly. She'd dreamed of making love with Simeon, but when she'd opened her eyes it wasn't her late husband's face staring down at her but Ryan Blackstone's.

She'd jumped out of bed, shaking uncontrollably as guilt assailed her. She'd been unfaithful to her husband's memory. It had taken half an hour before she fell asleep again only to be awakened by the same dream. This time she lay, savoring the pleasurable pulsing aftermath of her traitorous body.

Within minutes she succumbed to a sated sleep and woke at sunrise.

Leaving her bed, Kelly padded to the bathroom. Peering into the face in the mirror over the sink, she searched for a sign of shame or guilt, but found none. She had to face the realization that she was attracted to Ryan because she was a normal woman with normal sexual urges. At thirty she was much too young to permanently forego sexual gratification with a man. That was what her sister Pamela had tried to tell her. *I'm certain if you'd died instead of Simeon he wouldn't stop seeing other women,* Pamela had said repeatedly. *So why have you set yourself up as the martyred widow?*

I don't know, she had told Pamela over and over. And she hadn't known—not until now. What Pamela and Leo Porter and even she hadn't known at the time was that she had not met the right man.

But, was Dr. Ryan Blackstone the right man? "No," she said to her reflection.

She reached for a facial cloth in a small plastic container and wet it. Using a circular motion, she washed her face, then splashed cold water over her tingling skin before patting it dry with a fluffy towel. She filled the tub with water, adding a capful of perfumed oil, and brushed her teeth and tried to dismiss the erotic musing about a certain veterinarian from her mind.

* * *

Ryan raised his head to peer at the clock on the bedside table, groaning under his breath. It was minutes before three, and he hadn't had more than two hours of sleep since retiring for bed at ten-thirty. He knew the reason for his insomnia was Kelly Andrews.

It was as if he still could see the play of sunlight on her warm brown skin, the contrast of her white blouse against her velvety throat, and the lush curves of her hips in the slim skirt. What had surprised him was that she hadn't worn any makeup other than a soft shade of orange-brown lipstick, and still she was stunning.

Everything about her, from the way she'd dressed, her poise and the way she spoke screamed big-city sophistication. A wry smile curved his mouth, and Ryan wondered how long would it take before she tired of smelling hay, horse urine and manure. And when the weekends came would she be content to stay on the farm or would she head to the nearest big city for some *real fun?*

Throwing back the sheet, he sat up and left the bed, knowing he wasn't going back to sleep. Twenty minutes later, dressed in a plaid cotton shirt, jeans and a pair of old boots, he walked to the stables.

Sensors lit up the area where the prize horses were stabled for the night. Placing his right hand on a panel, he waited until a flashing red signal switched to a steady green before he punched in a code. The lock to the stable was deactivated. Sliding back a door, Ryan walked into the dimly lit space, and closed the door behind him.

He stopped at the stall of an exquisite foal, smiling at the potential Triple Crown winner. The colt, Shah Jahan, was the product of Blackstone Farms' winningest mare and a former Preakness winner. He had the bloodlines of a potential Thoroughbred champion.

Ryan lingered in the stable, checking on each horse, and when he walked out the workers were arriving with the rising sun. The build-up of heat had begun to burn away the haze covering the valley as he had made his way to his house, a weighted fatigue settling over him. His eyelids were drooping but he managed to shower before falling across his bed and into the comforting arms of Morpheus.

He slept deeply, not waking until late afternoon—well after the Blackstone Farms Day School's open house ended.

Kelly stood in the doorway to the brick structure, noting the curious expression on the face of a little girl. She was expecting a total of five children, ranging in ages from three to five. Two were brothers—identical twins Trent and Travis Smith. One glance at the redheaded, freckled, green-eyed twins signaled trouble—double trouble. Sean Blackstone,

Allison Cunningham and Heather Whitfield had also come to the open house. Delicate Heather had arrived first, her large brown eyes widening when she spied the area Kelly had set up as the house-keeping corner, followed by the twins, then Allison.

"You may go look at it," she urged in a gentle voice. Heather raced over to the play stove, turning knobs and stirring a pot with a wooden spoon.

Sheldon walked in with Sean clinging to his hand as if he feared his grandfather would disappear if he didn't hold on to him.

"Good morning, Sean." He stared up at Kelly, eyes wide.

"Miss Kelly spoke to you, Sean," Sheldon admonished.

"Good morning, Miss Kelly," he mumbled under his breath.

"Come in and join the others. We're going to have juice and cookies." Sean gave Sheldon a lingering look before he walked over to the other children gathering in the housekeeping corner.

Kelly smiled. "Please wait while I get the children settled."

Three women sat on a sofa and two of the four club chairs covered in supple black leather, talking quietly. A glass-topped black lacquered coffee table set on an area rug with a distinctive Asian motif in black and red mirrored the farm's silks. Solid brass floor lamps with pale linen shades completed the

inviting sitting area. Kelly planned to use this area
to meet with parents to discuss their children's pro-
gress or her concerns.

Sheldon sat down. His penetrating gaze swept
around the large space, cataloguing everything.
Flowering plants lined empty bookcases under a
wide window with southern exposure. A colorful
plush area rug with large letters of the alphabet covered the gleaming wood floor. An entertainment
center contained a wall-mounted, flat-screen television, VCR and DVD player. Oversized throw pillows were positioned on the floor in front of the
screen.

The science corner held a tank of colorful trop-
ical fish. Posters of farm animals, flowers, birds and
fish graced another wall. Cubbies with hooks and
the names of each child stood ready for sweaters,
coats and boots with the change of seasons. Half a
dozen portable cots were stacked against another
wall. He was amazed that it had taken Kelly only
a month to order the supplies and furnishings she
needed to set up her classroom.

He watched her firmly, yet gently, steer the five
children to a sink in a far corner. They washed their
hands and dried them on paper towels before racing
to a round table with half a dozen chairs. Each one
claimed a seat, waiting patiently as Kelly filled
plastic cups with apple juice and placed a large oat-
meal raisin cookie on the plate at each setting.

"After you finish your cookie and juice, you can watch a movie while I talk to your parents. Take your time, Travis," she admonished softly when he stuffed a large piece into his mouth.

Ten minutes later, cups and plates stacked on a tray for a return to the dining hall, the five children settled down on the large pillows to watch their movie.

Kelly walked over to the sitting area, joining the parents. Smiling, she said, "The Blackstone Farms Day School will open officially Monday morning, and I want to reassure you that your children will be exposed to a safe and positive environment while in my care...."

It was noon when the parents pulled their reluctant children away from the blank television screen, promising them they would come back in two days.

"Are you going to be here on Monday, Miss Kelly?" Sean asked.

She smiled at the expectant look on his face. "Of course I am, Sean. I'm going to be here for a very long time." She knew a year was a long time to a four-year-old. He smiled at her, his expression so much like his father's, and then skipped away to catch up with Sheldon.

Once everyone left, Kelly sat down on one of the club chairs, rested her feet on a corner of the coffee table, and closed her eyes. The open house had gone well. She waited half an hour, then began the task of unpacking and cataloguing books into a database of the personal computer Sheldon had given her for the school's use. It was later, well after the dinner hour when she slipped behind the wheel of her car and drove back to her house.

Kelly showered, changed into a pair of shorts and top, and then went into the kitchen to prepare her dinner, a small salad, which she devoured hungrily. She had just dried and put away her dishes when the doorbell rang. The sound startled her. It was the first time anyone had rung her bell. Drying her hands on a terry-cloth towel, she made her way out of the kitchen, through the parlor and to the door.

"Yes?" She had lived too many years in New York City to open the door before identifying who was behind it.

"Ryan."

The sound of his voice made her heart skip a beat before it settled back to a normal rhythm. "What do you want?"

"Open the door, Kelly," he said after a pregnant silence. "Please."

Her hand was steady as she unlocked the door, opened it and looked at Ryan staring at her as if he had never seen her before. It was only when she noticed the direction of his gaze that she realized her state of half-dress—a pair of too-tight, low-riding shorts and a revealing midriff top. The narrow waistband on her black lace bikini panties and the outline of her nipples under the white top were ardently displayed for his viewing.

Tilting her chin, she said, "What do you want?" she repeated. The question was filled with fatigue.

Ryan closed his eyes, but he still could see the soft curves of Kelly's body. Why was it whenever he met her one-on-one she was half-dressed?

He opened his eyes, forcing himself to look at her face and not below her neck. "I missed you at dinner. I just came by to check whether you'd eaten."

She nodded. "I had a salad."

He lifted a raven eyebrow. "Just a salad."

"I was too tired to fix anything else. I've had a long day."

"I thought I told you that you could order from the kitchen."

Kelly gave him a smile. "I know you did, but—"

"You're working too hard, Kelly."

"I'm not working too hard, Ryan," she countered. "I had a deadline to meet, and I met it."

He smiled, tiny lines fanning out around his eyes. "Congratulations. Do you want to celebrate?"

Vertical lines appeared between her eyes. "Celebrate?"

His smile vanished. "I'm certain you're familiar with the word."

"Celebrate how?"

He shrugged a shoulder. "Go into town."

Her gaze narrowed. "And do what?"

"Talk. If you want we could share a drink."

Kelly recalled her erotic dream earlier that morning and she fought the dynamic vitality Ryan exuded. She knew she wasn't immune to him, but she had no intention of permitting herself to fall under his sensual spell. She had come to this part of Virginia to teach, not become involved with a student's father or have an affair with her boss.

She offered him a conciliatory smile. "I'm flattered that you asked, but I'm afraid I have to decline. First of all, I'm tired. It's been a very exhausting week for me."

Ryan noticed the puffiness under her eyes for the first time. "And the second reason is?"

Her expression changed, hardening. "I've made it a rule not to *date* my boss." Much to Kelly's surprise, he threw back his head and let out a great peal of laughter. She frowned. "What's so funny?"

He sobered enough to say, "You."

"Me?"

"Yes, you, Kelly. Let me remind you that I'm not your boss. I didn't interview you, hire you or sign your contract. And that translates into my not being able to fire you. Only my father can do that." Crossing his arms over his chest, he angled his head. "Now, you're going to have to come up with another reason for rejecting my offer."

Bracing her hand on the door, she smiled. "That's an easy one." Without warning she closed the door and locked it. "Good night, Ryan," she said loud enough for him to hear.

Ryan stood motionless, staring at the door. She'd closed it in his face. "Well, I'll be damned," he whispered.

Kelly had called his offer to take her out a date while he thought of it as a meeting. Sean had come home that afternoon bubbling with excitement when he'd talked about his new school. It had been the most spontaneity he had seen in the child in over a year. He wanted to talk to Kelly about his son, but was he using Sean as an excuse to spend time with Kelly? In any case, meeting at her place was out of the question. The last thing he wanted was to generate gossip about the boss's son coming on to the new schoolteacher. As it was, there was enough gossip circulating around Blackstone Farms to fill a supermarket tabloid.

He chuckled in spite of his predicament. In that instant he realized he liked Kelly Andrews. He'd found her poised and beautiful. But he also knew she had a lot of fire under what she'd projected as a dignified demeanor.

Unknowingly she had issued a challenge when she closed the door in his face. And Ryan Blackstone had never walked away from a challenge.

Four

Kelly hadn't realized her hands were shaking until she picked up the telephone on the table beside her bed. At that moment she wanted to curse. She was pissed! And it wasn't Ryan she was angry at. She had become what she detested most: discourteous and ill-mannered.

Ryan had come to her, asking they go somewhere and talk. She hadn't even asked him what he had wanted to talk about before she slammed the door in his face.

Was she losing it because of an erotic dream?

Dialing the area code for Washington, D.C., she waited for the connection. She smiled upon hearing her sister's cheery greeting.

"Hi, Pam."

"Hey, Kelly. I hope you're calling to tell me that you have a date tonight."

She ignored the reference to a date. Even if she had gone out with Ryan she still would not have considered it a date. "I called to say hello to my big sister."

A groan came through the earpiece. "You called me last Saturday to say hello. What are you doing, Kelly? You've moved across the state and your social life hasn't changed. I think it would've been better if you had stayed in New York where you at least had a circle of friends."

"Married friends, Pamela."

"I know that, Kelly. But there's always the possibility that they could've hooked you up with a single friend or relative."

"I can always stop calling you—"

"I'm sorry," Pamela said, interrupting her. "I just got off the phone with Mama and Daddy. They've begun an intense campaign to try to make me feel guilty because I finally came out and told them that Leo and I decided not to have children. I don't know how much more of it I can take."

"Tell them that you don't want to discuss it."

"You try and tell Camille Kelly Andrews not to say what's on her mind."

Kelly smiled. Pamela was right. Camille may

have been outspoken and opinionated, but she was also fiercely supportive of her daughters.

"If she mentions it to me the next time we talk I'll be diplomatic when I tell her that you and Leo have a right to determine your own lives. That you're still a family even if you decide not to have children."

"Thank you, Kel," Pamela said, using her pet name for her younger sister.

The two sisters talked for another ten minutes, Pamela giving Kelly an update on her new position as an assistant curator at the National Gallery of Art. Leo, her husband, had taken over as curator at the National Museum of African Art two years before.

The first star had made its appearance in the sky when she stripped off her clothes and pulled a sheet over her nude body. This time when she went to sleep there were no erotic dreams to disturb her slumber.

Ryan's footfall was heavy as he made his up the porch steps to his father's house and sat down on a rocker across from the older man. Sean sat on his grandfather's lap, asleep.

"That was quick."

"It was quick because she wouldn't talk to me." Sheldon leaned forward. "Why not?"

"Why?" Ryan repeated. "I don't know why, Pop."

"What do you do to her?"

Stretching long legs out in front of him, Ryan crossed his feet at the ankles. "Nothing. I told her I wanted to talk to her and she closed the door in my face."

"Is that all?"

Ryan threw up a hand. "Is what all?"

"Why are you repeating everything I say?"

"Because I don't believe you're asking me these questions," Ryan shot back.

Recessed porch lights came on automatically in the waning light, flooding the space with beams of gold. It provided enough illumination for Sheldon to see a quivering muscle in Ryan's jaw.

"How did you look at her?"

Ryan struggled to contain his temper. "How does my looking at her have to do with anything?"

"Last night you looked at her as if she were dessert." He held up a hand when Ryan opened his mouth to refute his accusation. "You need to be gentle with her, son," Sheldon continued. There was a wistful quality to his voice.

Ryan decided to ignore his father's assessment of his reaction to Kelly as he stared at Sheldon, seeing what he unsuccessfully tried to conceal—pain. The last time he had seen pain in his father's eyes was the day Sheldon had buried his wife and the mother of his two sons.

"What happened to her, Pop?" he asked softly.

There was a noticeable pause and emerging nocturnal sounds were magnified in the silence. Sheldon sighed audibly. "She lost her husband a couple of years ago in a hit-and-run accident."

Ryan's eyes widened. He had no idea she was carrying that much emotional baggage. "How old is she?"

"Thirty."

A mysterious smile lifted the corners of Ryan's mouth when he recalled asking Kelly how old she was. He still thought she looked much younger than her age.

Sheldon glanced down at the small child sleeping on his lap. There were three generations of Blackstone men sitting on the porch and not one woman.

"Have you thought about remarrying and giving Sean a mother?"

"No more than you have when it came to giving Jeremy and me one."

Sheldon shook his head, smiling. "Touché, son."

"You've been widowed for twenty years, Pop. Don't you think it's time to let go?"

"I could say the same to you."

"No, you can't. Mom died. That's very different from dissolving a marriage."

"Do you ever think of remarrying?"

Ryan's eyes darkened until they appeared near black. "Yes and no. Yes, because I miss being part of an intact family unit, and no, because I have to think about Sean."

"Are you really thinking of him, Ryan? Both of you need a woman in your lives. How else will he learn to respect a woman if not from his father?

"I'm thinking only of him, Pop."

"The boy needs a *mother*, Ryan."

"People said the same to you when Mom died."

"That's true," Sheldon agreed. "The difference was you and Jeremy were fourteen and ten when Julia passed away. That's very different from a little boy who has no memories of his mother."

Ryan stared out into the night. He was so still he could have been carved out of granite. He knew his father was right, but knew he also was right. From the day he was born Sean had become the most important person in his life, and he made a pledge to never sacrifice the emotional well-being of his son for any woman.

Ryan stood at the window in his second-story bedroom early Monday morning, watching Kelly as she made her way to the stables. The last time he saw her had been Saturday night at her house. He had waited in the dining hall on Sunday, hoping to catch a glimpse of her, but she did not put in an appearance.

His eyes narrowed as he watched her knock on the door. It opened, and she disappeared behind it. Three grooms worked on a rotating basis once the stables were opened at sunrise to groom the eighteen horses before they were turned out to graze. The trainer and his assistants exercised the Thoroughbreds during the morning and early-afternoon hours.

What was she doing in the stable? Who was she meeting?

Turning away from the window, Ryan descended the staircase in a few long strides. He hadn't realized he was practically running until he felt his heart pumping rapidly in his chest. Taking a deep breath, he opened the stable door and walked inside.

An emotion he could only identify as relief swept over him when he saw Kelly rubbing Jahan's nose. She hadn't come to meet a man, but to see the horses.

"Beautiful."

Kelly jumped, turning to find Ryan standing behind her. It was the second time he had caught her off guard. She hadn't heard his approach over the sounds of a worker sweeping out a stall.

Turning back to the horse, she nodded. "That he is."

Ryan wanted to tell Kelly that he wasn't talking about Jahan. She looked scrumptious, casually dressed in a tank top and pair of jeans that showed every dip and curve of her tall, slender body. He stared at her feet.

"You should be wearing boots in here instead of running shoes."

"I don't have boots."

"Why not?"

"Because I haven't had the time to go buy a pair." She had spent Sunday restocking her pantry and refrigerator and putting up several loads of wash.

He moved closer. "Look at me, Kelly."

She went completely still. It had been only three days since she'd met Ryan for the first time, but the magnetism was definitely there. Something about him jolted her nervous system each time she met his gaze.

She wanted him even though she did not want to desire him, because in her head she wasn't quite ready to let go of the memory of her late husband. She had purposely avoided going to the dining hall, knowing Ryan would be there, so she continued to prepare her own meals at home.

"Why, Ryan?"

Resting his hands on her bare shoulders, he turned her to face him. "Because I want to look at you." He dropped his hands.

Her lashes fluttered before sweeping up to reveal what she so valiantly tried to conceal: her loneliness and a longing to be held and loved. Her gaze moved slowly over his face, lingering on his mouth. He wasn't wearing a hat, and his damp coal-black hair lay against his scalp in layered precision. His coloring, hair and features were a blending of races so evident in people in this region of the country.

"What do you see, Ryan?"

His dark gray eyes widened as they dropped from her steady gaze to her shoulders and chest. "I see an incredibly beautiful woman who in a few hours has worked wonders with my son." Sean had spent Saturday afternoon and all day Sunday asking when he was going back to school so that he could see Miss Kelly.

Kelly closed her eyes. It was not about her, but Sean. "He's a charming child."

Ryan wanted to tell his son's teacher that she had charmed him, too. He inclined his head. She tried stepping around him but he blocked her path.

"Why did you follow me in here? What is it you want from me?"

"I saw you from my bedroom window and I was curious as to why you'd come here so early. What is it I want from you?" He lifted a broad shoulder under a stark white T-shirt at the same time he shook his head. "I don't know, Kelly. That's something I haven't quite figured out."

Rising on tiptoe, she thrust her face close to his, close enough for him to feel her breath feather over his mouth. "Your homework assignment is to figure out what you want."

She pushed past him, heading for the door, but Ryan was quicker. He caught her arm, pulling her into an empty stall. "I want this," he whispered, seconds before his mouth covered hers in a hungry kiss that sucked the breath from her lungs.

His hands slipped up her arms, bringing her flush against him, and he deepened the kiss. Kelly put her arms around his neck to keep her balance, her soft curves melding with his lean length.

Her mouth burned with the pressure of his mouth moving over hers. The harsh, uneven rhythm of her breathing matched his; she was lost, drowning in the passion and the moment. It was only when she felt the probing of his searching tongue parting her lips that she pulled out of his embrace, gasping. The smoldering flame she saw in his eyes startled her. The lightning was out of the bottle.

Crossing his arms over his chest, Ryan angled his head. "I think that assignment deserves an A. What do you think, Miss Kelly?"

She placed her hands on her hips, ignoring the tingling sensations tightening her nipples. "I think you're disgustingly arrogant, Dr. Blackstone." She'd meant to insult him, but the breathlessness of the retort sounded like a compliment.

He smiled. ''I've been called worse.''

This time as she turned to walk out of the stables, he did not try to stop her. He followed, watching her straight back and the seductive sway of her hips.

''You owe me an apology, Miss Kelly.''

She stopped, not turning around. ''For what, Dr. Blackstone?''

''For closing your door in my face.''

Kelly pulled her lower lip between her teeth. It was obvious she was attracted to Ryan, and despite her verbal protests she wanted to see him. ''Share dinner with me tonight and I'll apologize properly.'' She glanced over her shoulder, seeing his shocked expression. A satisfied grin curved her mouth as she continued walking in the direction of her house.

Ryan knew he had shocked Kelly when he'd kissed her, but she had also surprised him when she'd held on to his neck.

There was a banked fire under Kelly Andrews's cool exterior. All he had to do was wait for the right time to re-ignite it. And something told him it would be good—not just for Kelly but also for him.

Kelly sat in the library corner with her students. All had eaten breakfast, cleaned up their table and were eagerly awaiting the first activity for their first day of school. Sitting on a stool, she smiled at their expectant expressions.

"Does anyone know what a calendar is?" Five hands went up. "Heather?"

"It tells days."

Kelly nodded. "Very good, Heather. What else can a calendar tell us?" She nodded to Sean, who hadn't lowered his hand.

"It tells weeks and months."

"We are going to use our calendar not only to tell us the date, but also for holidays, historic events, birthdays and special days, weeks and months. Today is May 23—World Turtle Day."

"I found a turtle," Travis announced proudly.

"Yeah, but Mama wouldn't let him keep it. She said it belonged outside," Trent countered before he stuck his tongue out at his twin.

Reaching for a picture book, Kelly opened it to an illustration of a turtle. "Your mother is right. Animals need to live in what it is called their natural habitat. The turtle is the only reptile that has a shell."

Allison pointed to the picture. "His shell is his house."

Sean raised his hand. "Miss Kelly, my daddy said a turtle can put his head, tail and legs inside his house when other animals want to eat him."

"Your dad's correct." Kelly was certain Sean knew more about animals than most children his age because Ryan was a veterinarian. She handed Trent a green felt cutout of a turtle with a Velcro backing. "Please put this on today's date under the heading of World Turtle Day. Can anyone tell what kind of weather we're having today?"

"Sunny!" They all had called out in unison.

Kelly picked up another cutout of a yellow oval shape with points circling it. "Heather, can you put up the sun?"

She jumped up. "Yes, Miss Kelly."

The morning hours passed quickly wherein Kelly showed the children how to hold paste scissors and cut animal shapes from a stencil. They put on smocks, painted their animals, placing them on a table to dry.

Lunch was delivered from the dining hall at exactly at noon, and an hour later three boys and two girls lay on cots in the darkened room, lying quietly until they all fell asleep.

The children were awakened at two-thirty and taken outside where they played an energetic game of tag and hide-and-seek. They stopped long enough for an afternoon snack of juice and nuts with raisins; they returned to the playground area, playing on the swings and teeter-totter. Their moods and interests changed quickly when they retrieved a jump rope from a large plastic bin.

Allison's mother came to pick her up, and Kelly enlisted her aid in helping to turn the rope as the children jumped while reciting the letters of the alphabet. None of them got past M before their feet got tangled in the rope's length.

Allison took the rope from Kelly. "Let me turn with Mommy while you jump, Miss Kelly."

Before Kelly could refuse all of the kids were chanting, "Jump, Miss Kelly. Jump, jump, jump!"

She remembered her childhood days when she'd jumped Double Dutch with her girlfriends during the summer months. The life span for a pair of her sneakers was usually two weeks.

Measuring the speed of the turning rope, Kelly jumped in. "A, B, C, D…" The children recited the alphabet as she jumped up and down as if she were ten instead of thirty. She heard Sean call Daddy and she faltered.

Standing less than five feet away was Ryan, grinning from ear to ear. He, not Sheldon, had come to pick up Sean.

"You win, Miss Kelly!" Heather shouted. "You got to *S*."

"My name starts with S," Sean crowed proudly, pumping his little fist in the air. He wrapped his arms around Ryan's waist. "We had lots of fun today, Daddy."

Ryan smiled at Kelly. "I think Miss Kelly had lots of fun, too."

"She did. We all did."

"Yeah!" chorused five young voices.

Allison hugged Kelly around her knees. "I will see you tomorrow, Miss Kelly."

She pulled one of the girl's curly dark braids. "You bet I will."

Allison left with her mother and Kelly stared at Ryan staring back at her. Something intense flared through his entrancement, sending waves of heat throughout her body. His stormy gray eyes stoked a banked fire.

Ryan reached for Sean's hand, his gaze fixed on Kelly's face. A hint of a smile softened his strong mouth, and he was not disappointed when she returned it with a mysterious one of her own.

"Daddy?"

"Yes, Sean."

"Do I have to go home now?"

Ryan tore his gaze away from Kelly to glance down at his son for the first time since arriving at the schoolhouse. "Yes. Miss Kelly is tired. She has to go home and get some rest so she can be ready for school tomorrow."

"Can't she come home with us? She can rest in my room."

"No, she can't."

"Why not?"

"Because…because…"

"Because Miss Kelly lives in her own house," Kelly said when Ryan did not complete his statement.

"Why can't she live with us, Daddy?"

"Let's go, Champ. We have to wash up before dinner." Even though he had spoken to Sean, he continued to stare at Kelly. "I'll see you later," he said in a quiet voice.

Kelly nodded. "Okay."

Ryan smiled the sensual smile she had come to look for. His smile was still in place when he led Sean toward a pickup truck. Kelly turned her attention to the remaining children, her pulse quickening when she thought of her promise to meet with Ryan later that night.

There was no doubt she was drawn to his sexual attractiveness, but was that enough? Was it enough to lessen the pain of loving and losing a man she'd loved all of her life? She had met Simeon Randall when both were assigned to the same first-grade class, and he had become her hero, protector. As they grew older she discovered and experienced passion in his arms and bed. A passion she did not know she had.

Simeon had offered her all the emotional and physical gratification and fulfillment she needed. And for the first time since she had come to Blackstone Farms she had to question whether she might be lucky enough to capture both again.

Five

Ryan hadn't realized he had been figuratively holding his breath until Kelly opened her door.

He knew he was staring at her like a star-struck adolescent, but he couldn't help himself. "You look very nice, Kelly."

Kelly smiled, opening the door wider. "Thank you, and please come in."

She knew she looked very different from the woman he'd seen jumping rope earlier that afternoon. Her hair, brushed off her face, was swept up in a twist on her nape. The sleek style was the perfect complement for a black cap-sleeved off-the-shoulder dress ending at her knees. A pair of sling back animal print leather sandals covered her bare feet.

She admitted to herself that he also looked very nice. A chocolate-brown jacket and matching slacks complemented a finely woven beige, banded-collar linen shirt.

His right hand concealed behind his back, Ryan walked into Kelly's home. The miniature Tiffany-style lamp on a round table cast a warm glow on exquisite antique pieces from another era. An apple-green armchair covered in a watered-silk fabric with a matching footstool was the perfect complement for a lavender-hued sofa dotted with light green sprigs. Classical music played softly from a stereo system hidden from view.

He followed her into the dining area, staring mutely at a table set for two. The crystal, china and silver patterns were exquisite. A multifaceted crystal vase held a bouquet of wispy sweet pea.

Kelly moved closer to Ryan, measuring his stunned expression. ''What are you hiding behind your back?''

He blinked several times before handing her a decorative shopping bag. ''This is for you.''

Kelly took the bag, peering inside. She walked over to a countertop and removed two bottles of chilled red and white wine and a cellophane-wrapped plant. Nestled in a hand-painted pot was a delicate orchid plant.

"It's beautiful, Ryan." Turning, she smiled at him. "Thank you so much."

Angling his head, he returned her smile. "You're welcome."

"We'll have the white wine because I'm making chicken." Grasping his hand, she steered him toward the sofa. "Please make yourself comfortable. Everything should be ready in about ten minutes."

He stopped suddenly, and she lost her balance and bumped into him. They stood motionless, her chest pressed against his arm. Ryan stared down at her under lowered lids. "May I help you with anything?"

Kelly wanted to tell him that he could help assuage the emptiness and loneliness that plagued her whenever she opened the door to the bungalow, or readied herself for bed. Everything that was Ryan Blackstone seeped into her at that moment: his height, the breadth of his shoulders, his penetrating eyes that saw everything, his haunting scent, his deep, drawling baritone voice and the virility that made him so confidently male.

"No, thank you," she said instead.

He held her gaze. "Are you sure, Kelly?"

She felt as if she were being sucked into a sensual vortex from which there was no escape. Kelly knew at that instant she had made a mistake. She never should've invited Ryan to dinner.

She wanted him! It was an awakening realization

that left her insides pulsing like the sensations from her erotic dream. And the harder she tried to ignore the truth the more it persisted. She was a normal woman with normal sexual urges.

She had cut herself off from people for two years. At Blackstone Farms she prepared her own meals instead of eating with the other employees in the dining hall. How long, she had to ask herself, was she going to continue to mourn for what was…what would never be again?

It was apparent Ryan was attracted to her—or why else would he have kissed her? And she could honestly admit to herself that she was very attracted to him. Why else would she have invited him to her home?

"Open the wine," she said as she turned and made her way to the kitchen.

A half-smile curved Ryan's mouth as he slipped out of his jacket and laid it over the armchair. Kelly wasn't as composed as she appeared. He had counted the fast beats of her pulse in her delicate throat. He had accepted her invitation because he wanted to spend time alone with her, not frighten her. He had never been one to come on heavy with any woman. If a woman rejected his advances then he retreated honorably.

The only exception was when he'd kissed Kelly in the stable. He'd told himself it was because she had challenged him, but he knew the instant his mouth had covered hers that it was what he'd wanted to do the first time he saw her lush mouth.

Ryan picked up a corkscrew off the countertop while Kelly removed a roasting pan from the oven. The mouthwatering aroma of baked chicken filled the kitchen. "No wonder you don't eat in the dining hall," he said, his gaze fixed on a golden-brown chicken surrounded by little cubes of roast potatoes.

He removed the cork from the wine bottle with a minimum of effort, watching as Kelly transferred the chicken to a platter, surrounding it with the potatoes and rosemary sprigs for a garnish. He washed his hands in the stainless steel sink, and dried them on a terry-cloth towel.

"I'll put that on the table," he said, taking the platter from her grasp.

Kelly emptied the juices from the chicken into a gravy boat, then removed a bowl of tossed greens, chopped celery, radishes and chives from the refrigerator. Reaching for a bottle of vinaigrette dressing she shook it over the salad.

Ryan took the salad bowl and gravy boat, placing them on the table before he pulled back a chair and seated Kelly. He lingered over her head longer than was necessary, inhaling the fragrance of her perfume. The scent claimed a subtle clean freshness bursting with a warm feminine sensuality.

His mother died after a long illness the year he'd turned fourteen, and although he could recall a lot of things about Julia Blackstone, it was her perfume that he remembered most. There was never a time when she hadn't smelled wonderful. She would say that just because she lived on a horse farm it didn't mean she had to smell like a horse. His mother loved the farm while his ex-wife had hated it. Sitting down across from Kelly he wondered whether she would be like Julia or Caroline.

Kelly smiled at Ryan. "Will you please carve the chicken?"

Picking up the carving knife and fork, he cut up the fowl with the skill he demonstrated in surgical procedures. He served her, then himself before filling their glasses with the wine.

Lifting his glass in a toast, he stared at the softness of his dining partner's lush mouth. "I offer you a very *special* welcome to Blackstone Farms."

Kelly lifted her glass, smiling at him over the rim. "And I accept your special welcome." Putting the glass to her lips, she took a sip. It was excellent. "The wine is wonderful."

Ryan nodded. After a bit of cajoling, he had gotten Cook to give him a bottle from his private stock. "Now that I've seen your home I see why you eat here instead of at the dining hall." He'd found her bungalow warm, inviting, and intimate.

"I eat here because once I come home and shower I'm usually too relaxed to get up and go out again."

"Are you tired now?"

She shook her head. "Not the exhausted kind of tired."

"I know I would be if I spent all day with five energetic kids."

Blushing, Kelly speared a portion of her salad. "How was your day?"

"Uneventful. And I can assure you that I did not have as much fun as you did."

After chewing and swallowing a portion of her salad, she said, "Uneventful as in boring?"

Ryan stared at Kelly, his expression impassive. He shook his head. "Do you find living on a horse farm boring?"

"It certainly hasn't been for me. I found setting up the schoolhouse a challenge, but after meeting the children I'd willingly do it all over again."

"You like teaching?"

"I love it."

"How about the children?"

"What about them?"

"Do you like children?"

Vertical lines appeared between her dark eyes. "Of course I like children. I love them."

"Why is it you haven't had any of your own?"

"I was waiting until I was thirty."

"How old are you now?" he asked, even though he knew.

"Thirty." She and Simeon had decided to wait

until they'd celebrated their fifth wedding anniversary before starting a family.

Ryan's hands stilled as his gaze fused with hers. "Have you selected the man who will father your child?"

"Not yet."

"Are you looking?"

"I wasn't."

"And now?"

Kelly took another sip of wine, choosing her words carefully. "Now that I've set up the school I'll have more time for a social life."

"You expect to find a baby's daddy at Blackstone Farms?"

"No, Ryan," she countered in a quiet voice. "If a man fathers my child, whether it is someone here or elsewhere, he will not be my baby's daddy but my husband."

He measured her with a cool appraising look, finding everything about her perfect. "Are you looking for candidates?"

Kelly laughed, the sound low, husky, and sensual. "Why, Ryan? Are you applying?"

His gray eyes darkened at the same time he lifted a shoulder. "Maybe."

She was shocked by the smoldering invitation in the gray pools. There was no doubt he was as physically attracted to her as she was to him. But it had to be more than sex. That she could get from any man. What Kelly wanted was love *and* passion. She concentrated on the food on the plate in front of her, feeling the heat from Ryan's gaze monitor her every motion.

"Well, Kelly?"

Her head came up. "Well what, Ryan?"

"Will you consider me as a candidate?"

"Why?" she asked, answering his question with one of her own.

He placed his hands, palms down, on the lace tablecloth. "Why? Because I like you—"

"But you don't know me," she said, interrupting him.

"And you don't know me. I only know what my father has told me about you. I know you're a widow and a teacher, while I'm a divorced father of a four-year-old son who wouldn't know his mother if she sat down next to him.

"I've never brought a woman around Sean because I know how much he wants a mother like the other kids. I don't want to give him false hopes that the woman his father is dating will become his new mother."

"And you're saying it would be different with us?"

Ryan nodded. "Yes. I could court you without Sean becoming confused about our relationship."

Kelly held up a hand. "Who said anything about a relationship?"

His eyes crinkled as he smiled. "There will never be a relationship if you won't let me court you."

"Why me and not some other woman, Ryan?"

"I don't know."

"We may see each a few times, then decide it's not going to work," she argued softly.

"If that's the case then we'll remain friends."

Kelly wanted to tell Ryan that women did not have male friends who looked like him. Either he would be a lover or nothing. What he was proposing sounded like a sterile business arrangement, but then wasn't that was what marriage was? It was an agreement between two people to love each other forever.

But she and Ryan did not love each other. They hardly knew each other. What she did have was a year in which to get to know him. And if it didn't work then she would leave Blackstone Farms Day School to teach somewhere else.

"Okay, Ryan. I'm willing to try it."

Pushing back his chair, he stood up and rounded the table. Curving a hand under Kelly's elbow, he pulled her gently to her feet. His large hand spanned her waist as he pulled her close.

He studied her upturned face, seeing indecision in her brown eyes. He hadn't lied to her. He did like her. Unknowingly she had shattered the barrier he had erected after Caroline rejected the child they'd created. Kelly had loved and lost like he had loved and lost. The difference was her loss had been final.

"I promise not to hurt you, Kelly."

She placed her fingertips over his mouth, while shaking her head. "No promises, Ryan."

"No promises," he whispered, repeating her plea. Lowering his head, he brushed his mouth over hers, sealing their agreement.

Kelly felt her breasts grow heavy against the hardness of his chest. If she had been in her right mind she would've questioned why she had just agreed to become involved with a man who was a stranger, a man on whose property she would live for the next year, and a man whose son was a student of hers.

All of her common sense dissipated like a puff of smoke as he staked his claim on her mouth and heart. She snuggled closer, leaving an imprint of her body on his. Ryan's hands moved from her waist to her hips, his splayed fingers pulling her against the solid bulge between his powerful thighs.

Pleasure, pure and explosive shook Kelly, leaving her trembling like a withered leaf in an icy blizzard when his tongue slipped between her lips. Her arms tightened around his neck, making him her willing prisoner.

Returning his kiss with reckless abandon, she moaned softly when he left her mouth to leave a series of light kisses down the column of her neck and over her shoulders. Eyes closed, head thrown back, she moaned again. The pulsing between her legs grew stronger and stronger, and she knew if she did not stop she would beg him to take her to her bed where she would play out her dream in the real world.

Somewhere, somehow she found the strength to pull out of Ryan's embrace. Her breasts were rising and falling heavily, bringing his gaze to linger on her chest. His head came up, and she bit down on her lower lip to keep from gasping aloud. The passion radiating from Ryan's eyes caused her knees to weaken. Reaching for her chair, she managed to sit without collapsing to the floor. He did not know her and she did not know him, yet the passion between them was strong and frightening.

Ryan sat down and picked up his wineglass, emptying it with one swallow. The cool liquid bathed his throat and body temporarily. He looked down at the delicious meal Kelly had prepared, unable to finish eating because she had lit a fire in him, a fire only she would be able to extinguish.

He wanted her in his bed, but he was willing to wait for her to come to him. After all, they had time, a lot of time....

Six

Kelly lay on a cushioned wicker love seat on the porch, her head resting on Ryan's chest. Raising her right leg, she wiggled her toes. She had left her sandals in the kitchen. She and Ryan had barely touched their dinner after the kiss. He'd helped her clear the table and wash and dry the dishes, and she'd suggested they sit out on the porch where it was safer than remaining indoors.

"What made you decide to become a veterinarian?"

Ryan rested his chin on the top of her head. "I've always loved horses and science, and becoming a vet was the logical choice. Also, I knew one day I would inherit the horse farm from my father, as it was with him and his father.''

"You'll be the third generation Blackstone to run the farm?''

"Yes. And hopefully Sean will become the fourth.''

"What about your brother?''

"Jeremy has no interest in horses. Pop refers to Jeremy as his vagabond progeny. My younger brother would lose his mind if he had to stay here more than a month.''

"How did the Blackstones become horse breeders?''

"My granddaddy was a white tobacco farmer who fell in love with a young black woman who had come to work for him as his cook. They couldn't marry or live openly as husband and wife because of Virginia's miscegenation laws. But she did give him a son. When James Blackstone died he left everything to Sheldon. Grandpa had grown tobacco for about twenty years, but after my grandmother died from lung cancer from a two-pack-a-day cigarette habit, he harvested his last tobacco crop and decided to raise horses.''

"Did he breed them to race?''

"No. He raised working breeds like the Welsh Cob, horses known for their hardiness and strength. He sold them to farmers and for riding. My father brought his first Thoroughbred several years after he'd married my mother. Within ten years he was racing competitively.''

What he did not tell Kelly was that his mother was an only child of a wealthy Charleston, South Carolina black family, and that his parents had used her inheritance to establish the largest and most successful African-American-owned horse farm in the state of Virginia.

''I know nothing about horses or racing,'' Kelly admitted. ''In fact, I've never been to a racetrack.''

Ryan's forehead furrowed. ''You've never watched our trainers exercising the horses?''

''No.''

''If you don't have anything planned for Saturday, then I'll have Kevin Manning show you how he trains horses for races.''

''Do you go to the races?''

Ryan hesitated. During his short marriage, the only time Caroline had deigned to grace him with her presence was at a horse race. ''Yes.''

Shifting slightly, Kelly gazed up at him. A shaft of sunlight hit his face, turning him into a statue of molten gold. Turning his head quickly, he glanced at her and she shuddered noticeably from the intensity of his stare. The large gray eyes glowed with an inner fire that ignited a spark of longing that left her gasping.

Ryan returned his gaze to the sprawling landscape in front of Kelly's bungalow. The homes for resident employees were constructed far enough apart to allow absolute privacy.

The fingers of his right hand traced the outline of Kelly's ear. "If I'd come back earlier I would've taken you to the Virginia Gold Cup. It's held the first Saturday in May at Great Meadow near The Plains. The Great Meadow also hosts the International Gold Cup the third Saturday in October."

"Isn't the Kentucky Derby run the first Saturday in May?"

He chuckled. "I thought you knew nothing about horseracing?"

"I do know the date for the Kentucky Derby," she said defensively. "How many winners has Blackstone Farms produced?"

Kelly listened intently as Ryan listed the races, the names of the horses and their jockeys who'd worn the black and red silks of Blackstone Farms into the winner circle. He explained domestic horses were bred in many different races and were grouped as ponies, heavy draft horses, lightweight draft and riding horses.

"Barbs and Arabs, the two most popular riding horses, originated from North African stock. Thoroughbreds are descended from Arabians."

She thought of the colt she went to see most mornings. "Jahan is the most exquisite horse I've ever seen."

"We call him our black diamond. Everyone connected with the farm believes he's going to become a champion.''

''What do you believe, Ryan?''

He wanted to tell Kelly that he liked her, liked her more than he dared admit. He wanted to tell her that something about her kept him a little off center. That he found himself thinking about her when he least expected. That he thought about her when he retired for bed and when he woke up.

''I believe if he stays healthy, he will stand in many a winner circle,'' he said instead. ''Have you ever ridden?''

''No.'' She laughed. ''Remember, I'm a city girl.''

''Do you want to learn?''

''Yes,'' she said, refusing to think of the consequences if she fell off a horse.

''Don't worry, we have a few Thoroughbreds with Irish Draught and native pony blood. They're less high-strung and more suitable for a novice rider like you.''

''Do the children ride?''

''Most of them sit a horse by the time they're walking. One of the boys who was born on the farm is now a jockey.''

''How old is he?''

''Nineteen.

Staring up at him, she gave him a saucy grin. ''By the way, how old are you?''

"Thirty-four."

"I suppose you're not too old to court me."

"How old did you think I was?"

"At least forty."

"No!"

"Well, you do have gray hair."

"Come on, Kelly, cut me some slack."

"That's hard when my first impression of you was that of a *doof* ball.

"Doof ball," he murmured under his breath. "Is that anything like a doofus?"

She nodded, clapping her hands. "Bravo! You just scored another A."

He glared down at her. "You've got a real smart mouth." Grasping her shoulders, he shifted her to sit on his lap. "If you play, then you have to pay. Are you prepared to pay, Kelly?"

She stared at him through her lashes. "That all depends on the game, Ryan."

He lowered his head. "Have you ever played *for keeps?*"

"No."

"Then I'm going to have to teach you," he whispered seconds before his mouth covered hers.

His kiss was slow, deliberate and methodical. It was gentle and persuasive. Healing. Exploratory. Drugging. Desire sang in Kelly's veins as she parted her lips, sampling and tasting the texture of the tongue exploring her mouth. His left hand moved up between her thighs, burning her bared flesh as her breathing deepened.

As quickly as it had begun it ended when he pulled back. And what she saw would be imprinted on her brain until she ceased breathing. The color in Ryan's eyes shimmered like a newly minted silver dollar. His eyes changed color with his moods, and instead of darkening with desire, his eyes turned into pools of liquid lightning.

Kelly tried to slow the runaway beating of her heart. "I think you'd better go *now* before we do something we may regret later." Her husky voice had lowered an octave.

Ryan slowly shook his head. "No, Kelly. I never do things I later regret."

Her senses were reeling as if her nervous system had been short-circuited by a powerful jolt of electricity. She hadn't known Ryan a week, yet he had lit a fire of desire she thought long dead.

Sitting upright, she pushed off his lap and stood up. Hands on her hips, she watched him stand. His body language was measured, precise. It was as if Ryan was in control of his life and everything in it.

Rising on tiptoe, she kissed his cheek. "I forgot something."

"What's that?"

"I forgot to apologize for closing the door in your face."

He lifted an eyebrow. ''There's no need to apologize.''

''But you told me you expected an apology.''

''That was before you agreed to date me.''

She nodded. ''Good night, Ryan.''

Bending over, he pressed a kiss under her ear. ''Good night, princess.''

He walked off the porch to where he had parked his car. He knew he had to slow down, not frighten Kelly. After all, they had a year to get to know each other.

I'm crazy. I've lost my mind, Kelly told herself over and over on the short drive to the schoolhouse. She had spent a restless night replaying her conversation with Ryan the night before.

She had also thought of herself as sensible and practical. When all of the girls she had grown up with were experimenting with alcohol, drugs and sex, it was Kelly Andrews who did not succumb to peer pressure. Why had she permitted Ryan to talk her into a situation in which she was not certain of the outcome?

She might be frustrated—after all, she was undergoing a sexual drought—but that did not mean she should contemplate sleeping with her boss's son. Kelly was certain she was certifiably *C-R-A-Z-Y!*

She parked her car and walked toward the entrance to the schoolhouse. Her step slowed when she saw a man at the door, waiting for her. Her car was the only one in the lot, which meant he had walked. She recognized his face, but not his name.

Smiling, Kelly said, "Good morning."

Snatching a battered straw hat from his head, he held it to his chest. "Good morning, Miss Kelly." He extended a hand. "I don't know if you remember me. Mark Charlesworth, ma'am."

She shook his hand. Although his clothes, his hands and clothes were clean, he smelled of the stables. "What can I do for you, Mark?"

He lowered his head, and a profusion of dreadlocks swept over his broad shoulders. "Can we talk, Miss Kelly? Inside?"

"Sure." She unlocked the door and pushed it open. A blast of hot air assaulted her as soon as she walked in. She had neglected to adjust the thermostat. Moving quickly, she pressed several buttons on a wall. Within seconds, the fan for the cooling system was activated.

"We can sit over there." Kelly gestured to the sitting area.

Mark followed Kelly, waiting until she sat down before he took a chair opposite her. Rolling the brim of his battered hat between long, brown fingers, he stared down at the floor.

Kelly waited for him to speak. The seconds ticked by. "Yes, Mark?"

His head came up and he stared at her with large, soulful dark eyes. "I need your help, Miss Kelly."

Leaning forward on her chair, she nodded. "How can I help you?"

"I want to go to college, but I don't know if I can pass the test the college says I need to get in."

She smiled. "You want me to tutor you?"

He smiled for the first time, showing a mouth filled with large white teeth. "Yes, ma'am."

"How old are you, Mark?"

"Twenty-two."

"Do you have a high school diploma?"

"Yes, ma'am. I dropped out at sixteen, but I went back and finished up last year. My dad said if I passed the test to get into a college he would pay for me to go."

"What do you want to be?"

He dropped his head again. "I'm not sure. I know I don't want to muck out stables for the rest of my life."

"Good for you." Kelly paused. "I'll help you."

Mark leaned forward and grasped her hands. "Thank you, Miss Kelly."

She winced as he increased the pressure on her fingers. "You can let go of my hand now." He released her hand, mumbling an apology. "If I'm going to tutor you, then it will have to be in the evenings."

He bobbed his head. "Yes, ma'am."

"Do you have any SAT practice books?"

"No, ma'am," he said quickly. "If you want I can pick up some."

"No, Mark. I'll buy them. I have an account with a company in Richmond that specializes in educational materials and equipment. I'll call and have the books sent to me at the school."

"But I'll still pay for it."

Shaking her head, Kelly said in a quiet voice, "Save your money, Mark. I'm certain Blackstone Farms will not be forced to file for bankruptcy because I charged a few review manuals to their account. As soon as they arrive I'll get in touch with you so we can arrange a schedule that will be conducive to both of us. Do you live here on the farm?"

"Yes, ma'am."

Kelly stood up, Mark rising with her. "I'll meet you in the dining hall, and we'll talk."

He closed his eyes, inhaled, and then let out his breath slowly. When he opened his eyes they were glistening with moisture. "I'd like to ask another favor, Miss Kelly."

She arched an eyebrow. "Ask."

He managed a sheepish grin. "I don't want anyone to know you're tutoring me."

Nodding, Kelly said, "It will remain our secret."

"Thank you, Miss Kelly."

"Thank me after you get an acceptance letter from a college."

"Thank you," he repeated before he turned on his heels and walked quickly out of the building.

Kelly felt a warm glow flow through her. She had come to Blackstone Farms to teach the preschool children of its employees, but there was nothing in her contract that precluded her extending her teaching skills to the farm's employees.

All of the children arrived by eight o'clock. They babbled excitedly about going swimming. Kelly had promised them the day before that if the morning temperature rose above seventy degrees, they could go swimming before lunch.

Sheldon motioned to Kelly. "I'll be bringing Sean for the next few days. Ryan had to take a mare to Richmond late last night for surgery."

"What happened?"

"He had to repair a bone spavin." Sheldon noted Kelly's puzzled expression, reminding himself she hadn't lived on the horse farm long enough to become familiar with equine terminology. "That's when there is an indefinite hind-lameness that shortens a horse's stride."

"Will she be all right?"

"Ryan says her chances of recovery are at least ninety percent."

"Ryan told me that all of the children ride."

Sheldon nodded. "But do they know exactly what everyone who works at the farm does?"

Sheldon's silver-colored eyes narrowed as he angled his head. "I don't know."

Kelly lifted her dimpled chin and smiled up at Sheldon, unaware of how attractive she was. "I'd like to set up a field trip. I'd like to take the children on a tour of the property to see firsthand what makes up a working horse farm. I want them to talk to the grooms, trainers, the people who put up and repair fences, cut the grass, muck out the stables and bale hay. I'd even like to give them a tour of the kitchen. It will help them to appreciate where they live and the importance of their parents' jobs."

Sheldon flashed one of his rare smiles. "Let me know when you want to do it, and I'll set it up."

"How about next week?"

"Monday is a holiday, so that's out. By the way, we always have big outdoor doings to celebrate Memorial Day, Fourth of July and Labor Day."

Kelly mentally filed this information. "What if we do it over four days? An hour for each presentation should be enough. Any more time than that will challenge their attention span, especially since they know everyone."

"You're right about that. Kids growing up on a farm tend to know a lot more than city kids when it comes to things like birth and reproduction, but we have strict rules about keeping kids away from the mares in heat. Seeing a stallion mount a mare can be an awesome sight for a child, especially if they believes he's hurting her.''

Waves of heat warmed Kelly's cheeks. She'd seen dogs and cats mate, but not horses. "Thanks for your cooperation.''

"Don't mention it,'' Sheldon said as he left.

One of the kitchen personnel walked in with breakfast, and the children raced over to the sink to wash their hands as Kelly smiled at her charges. They were so eager to learn and to please. She had bonded quickly with them, refusing to think of the time when she would be forced to let them go.

The wall telephone rang, and she rushed over to answer it. "Blackstone Day School, Miss Kelly speaking.''

"Good morning, Miss Kelly.''

Her heart leapt, turning over when she heard the deep, drawling voice. "Hi, Ryan.''

"How are you?''

"Good.'' She wanted to tell him she was very good now that she'd heard his voice. "Sheldon told me about the mare.''

"Peachy Keen is still in recovery, but I expect her to come through okay. She stopped racing several years ago, so we've used her exclusively for breeding purposes. Thankfully she has already foaled two colts, both of which could be potential winners.''

Kelly smiled. "That's good for Blackstone Farms."

"You've got that right. I'll probably be here until the end of the week. I want to wait to bring her back." There was a noticeable pause. "If you're not busy on Friday, I'd like to take you out for dinner."

Kelly wrinkled her nose. Ryan was asking her out. Finally her sister could stop haranguing her about not dating. "I have to check my calendar, but I believe I should be able to put aside a few hours for you Friday evening, Dr. Blackstone."

His sensual laugh came through the wire. "Still with the quick tongue? I believe I have the perfect remedy to take care of your tongue."

"Really?" she teased.

"Yes, *really*, Kelly."

"Hang up, Ryan."

"You first."

"Bye." Depressing the hook, she ended the call. A dreamy smile settled into her features, one that lingered throughout the day.

Seven

Sean sat on the padded bench at the foot of his father's bed, watching Ryan loop the length of a dark brown tie into a knot under the collar of a white shirt. "Do I have to sleep at Grandpa's tonight?"

Ryan caught his son's reflection in the mirror over a triple dresser. He tightened the tie, then turned to stare at Sean. "Yes, Sean."

The young boy stuck out his lower lip. "But, Daddy," he wailed.

"No whining, Sean. What is it you want?"

"I want to sleep over with Travis and Trent. They are having a Spider-Man party tonight."

"They may be having a party, but were you invited?"

"Yes, Daddy. They invited everybody from school. Even Miss Kelly."

Ryan studied his son's deeply tanned face and smiled. Sean had talked nonstop about what he did with Miss Kelly and the other kids at school during the time Ryan was in Richmond. He said he could read a lot of words, could count up to one hundred and match shapes and colors.

"Go get your sleeping bag while I call Miss Millie."

Sean jumped off the bench and raced out of the bedroom. Ryan picked up the telephone and dialed the number to the twins' house. Millicent Smith answered the call after the first ring.

"Hi, Millie. This is Ryan. I'm calling about the Spider-Man sleep over at your place tonight."

"Doc, I really need to have my head examined for agreeing to this," Millie drawled.

He smiled. "So, it's on?"

"Yeah. Drop Sean off at the dining hall and we'll bring him back with us."

"What time do you want me to pick him up in the morning?"

"Don't bother to pick him up. The kids don't have school tomorrow, and if the hot weather holds we'll probably hang out at the pool most of the day."

"You know if he gets to be too much for you just bring him back to Sheldon."

"Dr. Blackstone, you have the most well-behaved child on the farm. If my boys were half as good as Sean I'd consider myself blessed."

Ryan wanted to tell Millie that she *was* blessed. She had two bright, healthy sons. A parent couldn't ask for more than that. "They're boys, Millie."

"That's what Jim says. Thanks for letting Sean come."

"No problem, Millie."

"Bye, Doc."

Ryan rang off, then picked up the jacket to his suit, slipping his arms into the sleeves. He walked out of his bedroom and into Sean's across the hall. The boy was busy putting out changes of clothes on his bed. He watched as Sean took out socks, briefs, T-shirts and shorts.

Sean glanced up at his father. "Is that enough?"

Nodding, Ryan smiled. "Yes."

Sean picked up a backpack and put the clothes inside. After zipping the colorful bag, he hoisted it over one shoulder, then picked up a small duffel bag containing his sleeping bag.

"Are you ready, Champ?"

The little boy puffed out his narrow chest. "Yes, Daddy."

Ryan had taught Sean independence early. He had learned to select the clothes he would wear for the next day, laying them out the night before. He had to keep his room clean by picking up his toys and books. He knew he had to brush his teeth twice a day, wash his hands before and after meals, and say his prayers before he went to sleep.

Ryan cupped the back of his son's head, leading him down the staircase and out of the house. "I'm going to drop you off at Grandpa's."

Sean looked up at Ryan. "You're not going to eat with us?"

"No, Sean. I'm going out to eat."

"Who you eating with, Daddy?"

"Miss Kelly." He'd never lied to his son, and he did not want to begin now.

"She's pretty, Daddy. She's pretty like a princess."

"You're right about that, son."

"You like her, Daddy?"

"Yes, Sean, I like her."

"I like her, too. Isn't it good we both like her?"

"Yes it is."

Ryan wanted to tell Sean that what he felt for Kelly went beyond a simple liking. What he wanted was to see her—every day. He wanted to hold her close and feel her feminine heat, inhale her feminine fragrance. He wanted that and so much more.

He led Sean up the steps of the porch to the house where he'd grown up. The inner door stood open, as it did every day until Sheldon closed it to retire for the night. He held the screen door open for Sean.

"Grandpa!" Sean's strident voice echoed in the large living room.

Sheldon came from the direction of his study. It once had been called the family room. A network of lines fanned out around his eyes. He saw Sean's backpack and sleeping bag.

"Where are you going tonight?"

"I'm going to eat with you, then I'm sleeping over with Travis and Trent. We are going to have a Spider-Man party."

Sheldon's head came up and he stared at Ryan, who nodded. "Good for you."

Sean turned and stared at his father. "But Daddy's eating with Miss Kelly."

Sheldon angled his head, grinning. "Boo-yaw!"

"Boo-yaw to you, too," Ryan mumbled, while trying not to laugh. "I'll see you guys tomorrow."

"Have fun," Sheldon called out.

"Yeah, Daddy. Have fun with Miss Kelly."

Ryan walked out his father's house head high, and his step lighter than it had been in years. And it had been years since he really looked forward to sharing time with a woman, especially one as sexy as Kelly Andrews.

The week had passed quickly for Kelly and her students. They'd frolicked and splashed in the in-ground kiddie pool before they were served a picnic lunch under a large tent. Everyone napped, then swam again. When the parents came to pick up their sons and daughters later that afternoon all remarked how tanned and healthy they looked.

On Thursday Heather brought a kitten to school to show off her new pet. Miss Buttons had caused a stir when she jumped on the table to press her tiny nose against the fish tank. Kelly had to issue her first mandate: no pets in school.

It was now late Friday afternoon and she lay in the bathtub, eyes closed, and her hair wrapped in a silk scarf. A soft sponge pillow cradled her head. She had just completed her first full week teaching, and had almost forgotten how much energy it took to keep up with preschoolers. The only time they were still and quiet was at naptime.

The doorbell rang and she jumped, opening her eyes. "He can't be here!" she gasped. Ryan had called her earlier that afternoon to inform her he would come by to pick her up at six. Rising quickly, she stepped out of the tub, splashing water onto the tiled floor. She reached for a bath sheet, wrapped it around her wet body, and walked out of the bathroom.

She hadn't taken half a dozen steps when she saw him. Kelly sucked in her breath. Ryan stood in the middle of her parlor, dressed in an ecru-colored suit that made him look like a *GQ* cover model. His black hair was neatly brushed off his forehead and his deeply tanned gold-brown skin radiated good health. But it was his eyes—a smoky-gray that pulled her in and refused to let her go.

"Did you know that you left your door open?"

Her eyelids fluttered as she shook her head. She couldn't remember whether she had closed or locked the door. "I must be slipping. That never would've happened back in New York. By the way, what are you doing here so early?" Her voice had dropped to a whisper.

"I told you I'd be here at six."

"But…but it's not six."

Extending his left arm, the face on his timepiece showed beneath the starched cuff of his stark-white shirt. The hands indicated that it was exactly six o'clock.

Clutching the towel over her breasts, Kelly wrinkled her nose. "I'm sorry, Ryan. I must have lost track of time." She backpedaled, unable to believe she had fallen asleep in the bathtub. "Please excuse me while I put some clothes on."

A mysterious smiled curved Ryan's mouth. "Please…don't," he said in a quiet voice. "I happen to like what you're wearing."

Kelly stared at him. "I'm not wearing anything."

His eyes widened until she saw their sooty centers. "Exactly."

Her heart pounded an erratic rhythm as she

turned on her heel and rushed into her bedroom, slamming the door behind her. The clothes she had selected to wear lay across the bed.

Trying not to think of the man waiting in her parlor, she patted her body dry, moisturized her skin with a perfumed cream, dotted a matching scent at her pulse points, then slipped into her underwear and dress. It took another fifteen minutes to apply a powdered bronzer to the face, feather her eyebrows, apply a coat of mascara to her lashes and outline her mouth with a shimmering red lipstick.

She removed the scarf and pins holding her hairdo. Lowering her head, she brushed her hair forward off the nape of her neck and flipped it back until it settled into layered precision around her face and neck. Taking one last glance at her reflection in the mirror on the door inside the armoire, she slipped into her heels and picked up her evening purse. She walked into the parlor to find Ryan standing where she had left him.

It had taken only three days away from Kelly— only seventy-two hours for Ryan to realize how much he'd missed her. He knew nothing about her other than what he saw, but that was enough for him want her with an emotion that bordered on craving.

There was so much he wanted to share with her, yet he knew it was too soon in their relationship to make his desires known. He wasn't a boy, hadn't been one in twenty years, yet his need to share her bed exceeded any he had ever known in his life.

He watched her move closer, unable to take his gaze off her face and slender body that was showcased in a slim black tank dress. He measured each step she took in a pair of black, three-inch, sling strap sandals.

Moving closer, he placed his hand on her bared back. Peering over her shoulder he went suddenly still. He wasn't certain whether the back of the dress—what there was of it, began or ended just inches below the small of her back.

He grimaced at the same time he gritted his teeth. "Aren't you going to need a shawl or something for your shoulders?"

A smile trembled over her lips. "Nope.

"It might get cold."

She cut her eyes at him. "The temperature hit ninety today." Curving an arm through his, she smiled sweetly at him. "I'm sorry I made us late. Let's go."

"If any man looks sideways at you he's going to get a serious beat-down," Ryan mumbled under his breath.

Kelly frowned at him. "What did you say about a beat-down?"

"Nothing," he mumbled again, leading her to the door. Taking her keys from her hand, he closed and locked the door. He slipped the keys into the pocket of his trousers.

Ryan caught a glimpse of Kelly's bared back, admiring the silkiness of her dark brown skin. A lighter band of color showed beneath the narrow straps on her velvety shoulders. He smiled. It was obvious she had gone swimming with her students.

He opened the door to a low-slung two-seater black convertible sports car, waiting until Kelly was seated and belted in before he removed his jacket and placed it on the narrow space behind the seats. He sat down, put the key in the ignition, and the engine purred to life. Pressing a button he raised the top, adjusted the flow of cooling air coming through the vents, and pulled away from Kelly's home with a burst of speed.

Resting her head against the leather headrest, Kelly closed her eyes, enjoying the surge of power propelling the car forward. "Where are we going?"

"To an inn in West Virginia."

She opened her eyes and stared at Ryan's profile. "West Virginia?"

"It's not that far. It's a quaint little place in the mountains."

"Mountains as in Appalachian?"

"Yes, ma'am."

Those were the last two words they exchanged until more than an hour later Ryan maneuvered into a parking lot of a hotel and restaurant that had been built into the side of a mountain.

A valet opened the driver side door for Ryan, handing him a ticket while Ryan reached for his jacket, putting it on as he came around to assist Kelly. His right arm curved around her waist and he led her to the entrance of the restaurant.

Kelly felt as if she had stepped back into the nineteenth century when she surveyed the Victorian furnishings. The maître d' directed them to a table in a corner where a quartet of large painted urns provided a modicum of privacy.

Ryan ignored the menu and wine listing on the table; he stared at Kelly's face in the golden glow of flickering candlelight. The nostrils of his aquiline nose flared slightly. "Did I tell you how beautiful you look tonight?" Her lids lowered, the demure gesture enchanting him.

"No." She glanced up, meeting his heated gaze. "But you could've told me that back at the house."

"No, I couldn't, Kelly."

"Why not?"

"Because I don't think we would've left the house."

Unconsciously her brow furrowed. "What are you talking about?"

"I would've asked if you would let me make love to you."

She gasped softly. "Is that what you want to do, Ryan? Make love to me?"

Reaching across the table, he captured her hands. "Yes."

Kelly felt her stomach muscles contract. There was so much passion in the single word that she found it hard to swallow. Her breasts rose and fell heavily, bringing his gaze to linger there.

Could she tell him? Did she dare reveal what lay in her heart? That she also wanted him. Had wanted him the first time he'd held her in his arms after she had fallen off the stepladder.

"I do, too," she admitted in a voice so soft Ryan found it difficult to believe what he was hearing. "However, there is a part of me that says becoming physically involved with you will change me, change everything."

He tightened his grip on her fingers. "How, Kelly?"

"I...I don't want to forget Simeon. And I know once I sleep with you he will no longer exist for me."

"Simeon is your late husband?" She nodded. "Do you still love him?"

She smiled a sad smile. "I'll always love him."

"There's nothing wrong in loving him. But he's gone. And if he loved you as much as you loved him, then I believe he would want you to be happy."

Moisture shimmered in her eyes. "Do you think you can you make me happy, Ryan?"

He made love to her with his eyes. "Only you can make that possible."

Kelly shook her head. "I don't understand."

"Not only do you have to love with your head, but also with your heart. Loving has to be both, not one or the other."

She sniffled, and Ryan reached into a pocket and produced a snow-white handkerchief. Moving his chair closer to hers, he held her chin and dabbed her eyes. Resting his forehead against hers, he kissed the end of her nose.

"You're not the only one hurting, princess. I've been there, too. I fell in love with a girl I'd met in college. After graduating we went our separate ways, then one day out of the blue she called me. I invited her to the farm and she was caught up in the prerace excitement and parties. Blackstone Farms had entered a horse in the Virginia Gold Cup. Miss Fancy Pants was a twenty-to-one long shot, but we still had a lot of faith in her because she had heart. Our horse won, and that night Pop threw a party to end all parties. Caroline and I celebrated in our own special way, and the next day we announced our engagement.

"We had a September wedding, and by December she discovered she was pregnant. That's when everything changed. She became depressed and talked about aborting the baby." Ryan ignored Kelly's audible inhalation. "I was forced to watch her around the clock because I thought she was going to…" His words trailed off.

"Take her own life," Kelly said softly, completing his statement.

He nodded. "She said she hated me and hated living on the farm. She cried that she was being smothered to death and wanted to go back to Los Angeles. Caroline carried to term, but when she went into labor she made me promise to either give her a divorce or she would kill herself. I know I probably could've had her committed, but I agreed on one condition. She could leave, but she could not take my son. I refused to jeopardize his life with a woman who had proven herself to be emotionally unstable.

"I had my lawyer draw up the agreement before she left the hospital. Sean was two months old when she got into her car and drove away. I loved her, Kelly. Loved her enough to let her go so that she could find her happiness."

Kelly laid her head on Ryan's shoulder. "You've had your share of pain."

Curving an arm around her bare shoulder, he pulled her closer. "That's true, but I've learned not to wallow in it. There comes a time for healing."

Kelly knew he was talking about her. She had

been wallowing in her pain for two years, accepting it as readily as breathing and sleeping.

"You want me, Ryan, knowing I'm still carrying baggage? Knowing that I'm not ready to offer you what you feel you deserve from a woman?" She sucked in her breath. "I haven't slept with a man in two years, and what I miss most is the intimacy." There was a sob in her voice. "Are you willing to accept me giving you my body without offering my heart?"

Ryan waved back, his gaze meeting her tortured one. He did want her, more than any other woman in his past. "You fascinate me, Kelly," he confessed. "I don't know whether it is your beauty, spunk or your intelligence. And I have no right to demand or expect you to offer me anything. What I will accept is anything you're willing to give me."

Her lids slipped down over her eyes as her lips parted. Ryan angled his head and slanted a kiss on her mouth, silently acknowledging the terms of their agreement. The kiss ended and they exchanged a knowing smile.

Ryan blew out his breath. "I don't know about you, but I could use a drink right about now."

Closing her eyes, Kelly sighed softly. "I could use one, too."

Eight

"An apple martini?"

Kelly rested her chin on the heel of her hand. "Yes, Ryan, an apple martini. It's the rage in New York City."

He stared at her animated features, smiling. The tears that had filled her eyes when she had spoken about her late husband had vanished. They had reached the point where their relationship had to be resolved. Kelly wanted him to make love to her, and he would but only when the time was right. What he did not want was anything planned or staged. He wanted spontaneity.

Curving a hand around her neck, he wound his

fingers through her hair. "It must be a girlie girl concoction. A real martini is vodka or gin, not some sissy-tasting apple liqueur."

Smiling up at him through her lashes, Kelly shook her head. "Girlie girl?"

"Yes," he whispered against her lips. "You are the ultimate girlie girl."

"I stopped being a girl a long time ago," she crooned.

Ryan's hand went from her neck to her back. His fingers trailed down her spine, eliciting a shudder from her. "Wrong, princess. You're a woman-girl." He lowered his head and kissed the nape of her scented neck.

His mouth longed to follow the direction of his hand down the length of her spine. He wanted to taste Kelly—all over—until he gorged on her lush flesh.

Kelly felt the heat from Ryan's body seep into hers, it igniting an inferno between her legs. Her body began to vibrate with liquid fire, and she gasped softly as her flesh pulsed with a need that bordered on insanity.

Ryan's sensitive nostrils caught the scent of her rising passion, and he stared at the sensuality parting her full lips and dilating her pupils. Their waiter approached the table, carrying their drink order.

Kelly barely noticed the waiter placing her drink in front of her because the hardness of the thigh brushing against hers. Her whole being was flooded with a desire she hadn't known she possessed. *It's been a long time,* she mused. It had been a long time since the mere presence of a man had her quaking with desire.

Reaching for the icy glass with the pale green liquid, Ryan took a sip of Kelly's drink. It slid down his throat, cooling it before a warming spread in his chest. "Nice."

She picked up his tumbler filled with the concoctions for a Rob Roy, taking furtive sips. She grimaced. "Now, that's strong."

Handing Kelly her martini, he said, "It's definitely not Kool-Aid." He put the tumbler to his lips and drank deeply.

"Ryan?" Her voice was a mere whisper.

"Yes."

"Do we have to eat here?"

His sweeping eyebrows lifted. "Where do you want to eat?"

"Upstairs."

"You want to check into a room?"

She gave him a long, penetrating stare. "Yes."

Long, black lashes concealed the intensity in his gunmetal-gray eyes as he nodded. "Wait here while I register at the desk."

Kelly nodded, then slumped back to the cushioned softness of her chair. It was about to begin. She was ready to move forward, turn a corner and leave her past behind her. She would always love Simeon, but she knew she had to take a chance at finding love again, and that would only become possible if she looked forward. She had finished her drink when Ryan returned.

He helped her to her feet, cradling her against his side as he led her toward the elevator. His large hand covered the small of her back, fingers splayed over the roundness of her hips.

A tall, flaxen-haired man who looked as if he'd just left an Icelandic ski slope joined them at the elevator. Rocking back on his heels, he stared at Kelly's bared back. *"D-a-a-m-n-n!"* he gasped, drawing out the word.

Ryan's head snapped around, and he glared at the blond giant. "What's up?"

The man put up his hands at the same time he shook his head. "Nothing, man."

Dropping his arm, Ryan took off his jacket and draped it over Kelly's shoulders. The doors to the elevator opened and he escorted her into the car. He gave the man a narrow stare. "Aren't you coming?"

Kelly's admirer shook his head. "No. I'll wait for it to come down."

Ryan punched a button for the fourth floor. "Suit yourself."

Waiting until the doors closed, Kelly stared at

Ryan as if he were a stranger. "What was that all about?"

Staring straight ahead, he said, "Nothing."

"Were you calling that man out?"

"Nope."

Shrugging off his jacket she handed it to him. "I'm not cold, thank you very much."

The doors opened with a soft swooshing sound, and Ryan reached for Kelly's hand. They walked the length of the carpeted hallway to a room at the end of the hall. A brass plate on the door read Skyline. He inserted the magnetic card in a slot and seconds later he opened a door to reveal an opulent suite of rooms.

This suite was designed with walls made entirely of glass. The view through the glass of the Appalachian Mountains and forested areas was breathtaking. Ryan dropped his jacket over the back of chair in the entryway.

Leaning against Ryan, Kelly bent down and slipped off her heels. Her toes disappeared in the deep pile of the plush gold carpeting. She turned into his embrace, sighing as he pulled her to his chest. Tilting her head, she smiled up at him. "It's beautiful."

The corners of his mouth curved in a half smile. "You are beautiful, Kelly."

Rising on tiptoe, she pressed her mouth to his,

tasting the liquor on his lips. He deepened the kiss, his tongue slipping into her mouth.

Ryan's hands moved to cradle her round face between his palms; he willed himself to go slow. It had been a while since he had shared his bed with a woman, but nowhere as long as it had been for Kelly and a man. He left nibbling, teasing kisses at the corners of her mouth, over her eyes, along the length of her neck. His lips feather-touched her throat.

"I want you so much," he moaned against her ear.

Kelly clung to Ryan's neck like a drowning swimmer. "Then take me," she whispered hoarsely.

Bending slightly, Ryan scooped Kelly up into his arms, carrying her through the sitting room and into a bedroom with a king-size bed. The shimmering glow of the setting sun coming through the wall of glass threw shadows across the bed. Outside the shadows covering the mountains and valleys were reminiscent of the landscape pictures painted by the artists from the Hudson River School.

Cradling Kelly with one arm, Ryan pulled back a duvet and lightweight blanket to reveal a pale-yellow sheet. He lowered her gently to the mattress, his body following hers down. Gazing deeply into her clear-brown eyes, he smiled. Glints of gold sparkled as she gave him a shy smile.

He returned her smile. "I want it to be good between us." He needed it to be good because...he was falling in love with Kelly.

"Being here with you, having you hold me is good."

His fingers traced the outline of her delicate jaw. "Don't worry about anything. I'll protect and take care of you."

She wasn't certain what he meant by the cryptic statement, but mentally dismissed it as he slipped his hands under the straps on her shoulders, easing them down and off her arms and gasping softly when he stared at her naked breasts rising and falling above her rib cage.

Her breasts were perfect. Not too large or small, they were tipped with dark chocolate-brown nipples. He undressed her slowly, his gaze burning her flesh everywhere it touched. Sitting back on his heels, he removed her dress and black lace bikini panties. Everything about her body was alluring. From her flat belly, curvy hips and long shapely legs to her flawless brown skin that gave the appearance of whipped mousse.

Kelly forced herself not to cover her body with her hands, because there was something about the way Ryan was staring at her nakedness that made her uncomfortable. Rising off the mattress, she went to her knees. "Now, it's my turn," she whispered, her mouth touching his.

Ryan did not move, not even his eyes, as he permitted Kelly to undress him. His breathing quickened as she slipped off his tie and unbuttoned his shirt. Moving closer, her breasts touching his chest, she reached up and pushed the shirt off his shoulders. He did close his eyes once she unbuckled the belt around his waist. By the time she undid the waistband and unzipped his trousers, he felt the constriction in his chest.

Kelly felt the rising heat from Ryan's body like the steam in a sauna. It intensified the natural masculine scent and the sensual fragrance of his cologne. He pushed her hands away, slipped off the bed and finished undressing.

She stared at the broad expanse of his chest covered with a profusion of black hair. Seeing Ryan like this reminded her of how different he was from Simeon. Wherein Simeon was only several inches taller than she was, Ryan exceeded her five-foot, eight-inch height by at least six inches. Simeon's coloring was dark, while Ryan's was golden-brown. Simeon's body was smooth, unlike the crisp black hair covering Ryan's chest, arms and legs.

She would not let her gaze venture below his waist after she'd glimpsed the thick, heavy organ nestled between his powerful thighs. Ryan wasn't fully aroused, yet he was huge! The mattress dipped when he joined her on the bed. She closed her eyes.

Ryan eased her down to a pillow. "Look at me,

darling.'' She complied and slowly opened her eyes. Curving his arms around her waist, he shifted her until she lay over his chest, her legs nestled between his. Moaning softly, Kelly buried her face between his neck and shoulder.

''Tell me what you me want to do,'' he said in her hair. ''Tell me what I have to do to make you feel good.''

Kelly felt tears prick the backs of her eyelids. Simeon had been the only man she had slept with, and never had he asked what she'd wanted in bed.

''I don't know.'' Her voice was soft and child-like.

Ryan smiled. ''Do you want me to kiss your body?''

''Yes.''

''All over?''

''Yes.''

''Do you want to be on top or underneath me?''

It was her turn to smile. ''Both.''

''Front or rear?'' She gasped, and he laughed, the sound coming from deep within his broad chest. ''We'll save the rear position for another time.''

Reversing their positions, he supported his weight on his elbows. He closed his eyes and lowered his head, brushing a kiss over her mouth and leaving it burning with heat. Kelly found his mouth warm and sweet, moving with a slow, drugging intimacy that left both trembling.

Nothing was rushed. Not the shivering kisses starting between her breasts and trailing lower to her belly. Not his teeth nipping her nipples, turning them into hard buttons. But once he placed his hands against the inside of her thighs, spreading them wider, the sensual assault began.

She arched off the mattress as he searched for the tiny bud of flesh between her legs, and once finding it he laved it with his tongue until it hardened and swelled twice its size.

Kelly gripped the sheets, swallowing the moans trapped in her throat. Ryan's mouth and tongue played havoc with her nerve endings as she struggled not to climax.

Cupping her buttocks in both hands, Ryan raised her hips and plunged his tongue into her quivering flesh and drank deeply. He felt Kelly trembling, heard her soft pleas for him to stop, but he ignored her.

It was his intent to brand her with his possession, to make her forget all other men ever existed. He wanted to be the last man in her bed and in her life.

Kelly felt as if she stood outside of herself, watching herself float to a place where she'd never been. The desire streaking through her body was strange and frightening.

''No,'' she gasped, her head thrashing from side to side. She didn't want to feel this way, unable to control what was happening to her. "Ryan, please stop."

He did stop, but only long enough only to open the packet containing a condom he had taken from the pocket of his trousers. He rolled it down his tumescence, moved her over again and guided his engorged sex into her body.

Ryan kissed Kelly's taut nipples, rousing her passion all over again. She groaned with each inch that disappeared into the folds of her pulsing flesh. Once fully engulfed in her heat, he began to move.

Slowly.

Deliberately.

Pulling out.

Pushing in.

Pulling out a little more.

Pushing in a little harder until he established a rhythm that had them both moaning in ecstasy and gasping for their next breath. She rose to meet his powerful thrusts, their bodies in exquisite harmony with one another.

Opening her mouth, Kelly gasped in sweet agony as she felt the waves sweeping over her increase. The pleasure Ryan offered her was pure and explosive. He quickened his movements, his head buried between her neck and shoulders, and it was then that she cried out as love flowed through her like liquid heat.

She climaxed once, twice, then lost count as she

was hurtled to another dimension. She lay drowning in the aftermath of her sensual journey when Ryan exploded, his deep moans of ecstasy echoing in her ear.

He collapsed on her and she welcomed his weight and strength. Their shared moment of ecstasy had passed, yet she was filled with an amazing sense of fulfillment.

Wrapping his arms around Kelly's waist, Ryan reversed their positions and smiled. Her face was moist, her mouth swollen from his kisses. He lifted his eyebrows. "Did I hurt you?"

Kelly stared down into the gray eyes that reminded her of streaks of lightning across a summer sky. "No." And he hadn't hurt her. However, she was certain muscles she hadn't used in a while would be a little sore.

Resting her head on his shoulder, she snuggled closer. She could feel the heat of his large body course down the length of hers. "Thank you, Ryan."

"For what, darling?" His hand moved up and down her spine in a comforting motion.

"For reminding me what it means to feel like a woman again."

He dropped a kiss on her mussed hair. "If I make you feel womanly it's because this is the first time in a long time I'm glad that I was born a man."

Raising her head, she stared at him staring down

at her under lowered lids. He was so handsome that she found herself speechless for several seconds.

"I'm glad I waited."

His arm tightened around her waist. He wanted to tell her that he was glad he had waited for her. Reaching over to his right, he picked up the watch he had left on the bedside table. It was after eight. "Are you hungry?"

"Starved."

"I'll call and have our dinner sent up."

Kelly pulled out of his embrace and sat up. "I need to take a shower first."

Grinning, he reached for her hand. "We'll save time by sharing one."

She gave him a knowing look. "No seconds before we eat."

"I don't know what you're talking about. I already ate."

Kelly slapped playfully at Ryan, missing his shoulder when he ducked. He swept her up, throwing her over his shoulder as he headed toward the bathroom.

They shared a shower, Kelly complaining because he had ruined her hairdo when he held her under the flowing water while kissing her until she pleaded with him to let her go.

Wrapping her wet hair with a towel, she dried her body from a supply of thick, thirsty towels in a closet in the spacious modern bathroom. The closet yielded bathrobes and terry-cloth slippers in varying sizes.

Two hours later, she sat on a love seat in the dining area, her bare feet resting on Ryan's thighs. They had turned off all the lights, lit several candles and turned on the radio to a station that played mostly slow love songs.

She patted her belly under the terry robe. "I ate too much."

Resting the back of his head on the love seat, Ryan said, "Nonsense. I ate more than you did."

They'd devoured a platter of marinated asparagus, artichoke, grilled peppers, steak tidbits and grilled shrimp.

"That's because you ate faster than me."

"True," he said, lifting a flute of champagne.

Kelly raised her own flute, sipping the bubbling liquid. She hadn't finished her first glass. "What time do you plan to drive back?"

"What makes you think I'm driving back tonight?"

She could not make out his expression in the shadowy darkness. Sitting up straighter, she said, "What are you talking about?"

Ryan put his flute down on the table. "Unless you have another engagement this evening, I don't see the need to leave."

"What about Sean?"

"What about him?"

"Wouldn't he…"

"Wouldn't he what?" Ryan asked when she did not finish her question. "I'm not neglecting my son, Kelly, if that's what you're concerned about. He's spending the night with the Smith twins. They're having a Spider-Man party."

Heat flared in her cheeks. "I just don't—don't want to be responsible for keeping you from your son."

He curved his fingers around her slender ankles, holding her fast. "That could never happen. I've assumed total responsibility for Sean from the first time he drew breath, and there has never been a time when I've neglected him. I may not have always made the right decisions where it concerned him, but I've done the best I could.

"Sheldon begged me not to take him with me when I went to Tuskegee, but there was no way I could leave him for almost a year even though I knew he would be well cared for at the farm. Sean sulked the entire time he was away. He acted out because he didn't want to go to the daycare center whenever I taught a class, and he refused to talk to me whenever I came to pick him up. I made a mistake because I thought I knew what was best for my son. That was one time when I was thinking only of myself, but that will never happen again."

Kelly put her flute next to Ryan's, then leaned

forward to curve her arms around his neck. "No one is born a parent. We learn through trial and error. But in the end you will find that you've done a pretty good job." She kissed his chin. "Sean will grow up to be as proud of you as you are of Sheldon."

He nodded. "Pop and I sometime have our differences, but if I turn out to be half the father he is then I'll be more than grateful. It wasn't easy for him when Mom died, leaving him with two boys who thought they knew more than he did. He was still pretty young when he became a widower, but he refused to remarry because he said he did not want another woman believing she could replace his sons' mother."

"How old were you when your mother passed away?"

"Fourteen. Jeremy had just turned ten. We were so angry, unable to accept that our mother was gone. I'm ashamed to say that we gave Pop hell for a few years until he said he wouldn't treat us like men until we started acting like men."

"Did you straighten out?"

"I'm still here, aren't I?"

"Were you and your brother *that* out of control?"

"We weren't what you would call thugs or criminals, but we never walked away from a fight. I wasn't as bad as Jeremy, but I had to back him up because he was my brother.''

''You haven't changed that much, Ryan.''

His forehead creased in a frown. ''Why would you say that?''

''You were looking to start something with that guy at the elevator.'' He let go of her legs, picked up his flute, and took a swallow. She peered closely at him. ''And because you're not saying anything let's me know that you're still a brawler.''

He lifted an eyebrow. ''It wouldn't have come to anything, Kelly.''

''Why?''

''I'd never let you see me act like that.''

''But are you still capable of brawling?''

''Sure. But I'd rather make love.'' He put aside his flute and reached for her. He untied the belt holding her robe together, running a hand up her inner thigh.

A moan slipped past her lips. ''Ryan.''

''Yes, baby,'' he whispered in her ear.

She moaned again. ''That's not fair.''

''What's not fair, princess?''

''You're taking advantage of me.''

He chuckled. ''You can always take advantage of me.''

Kelly reciprocated as her hand searched under his robe to find him hard and ready. ''What are you waiting for? Let's go back to bed.''

This time there was no prolonged foreplay as Ryan paused long enough to slip on a condom, then entered Kelly's pulsing body and sent shivers of delight through her.

Their lovemaking was strong and passionate, each striving to delay fulfillment until the last possible moment. But they were not to be denied as they used every inch of the large bed in their quest to touch heaven. They exploded together, incinerating in flames of passion that burned long after they fell asleep entwined in each other's embrace.

Nine

Kelly returned to Blackstone Farms Saturday morning with Ryan, wrapped in a cocoon of contentment. She woke up to find him lying on his side, his head resting on a folded arm, smiling at her. They had not made love again, but lay in bed for several hours talking. She told him how it had been to grow up in New York City and how different Virginia was from the fast pace of a city that never slept.

Ryan had revealed that he'd visited New York twice, both times for professional conferences. He said he'd been shocked by the number of people crowding into a single subway car, but admitted that while he loved the pulsing excitement he knew he could never survive living in a big city. After a wonderfully long night, they'd finally left the bed, showered and eaten breakfast in their suite before checking out.

Kelly stood on the porch to her house, a hand resting in the middle of Ryan's chest. "Pick me up at one." He'd promised to take her into Staunton where she could buy a pair of riding boots.

Lowering his head, he kissed her tenderly. "I'll see you later." He smiled, turned and walked back to his car.

She unlocked the door and was met with the shrill ringing of the telephone. Rushing into the bedroom, she picked up the receiver before the answering machine switched on. A blinking number indicated two calls had been recorded.

"Hello."

"Where have you been? I've been trying to reach you since last night. I left two messages on your machine. Leo had to talk me out of driving across the state to find out what happened to you."

Kelly smiled as she kicked off her shoes. "I didn't know I was on work-release this weekend."

"Very funny, Kel."

"You bitch and moan when I call you every Friday or Saturday night, and when I don't you overreact."

There was a pulse beat of silence before Pamela's

voice came through the wire again. "You had a date?"

"Yes, I had a date." Kelly held the receiver away from her ear as her sister let out an ear-piercing shriek.

"Who is he? Where did you go? What did you do?"

"Dang, Pamela."

"You can say damn, Kelly."

"All right. Damn, Pamela."

"You don't have to tell me what you did," she said. "But you have to tell me who he is."

"His name is Ryan Blackstone."

"He's one of the Blackstones?"

"He's the eldest son."

"Hot damn! My little sister struck the mother lode."

"Back it up, Pamela. It was just one date."

"One, two, three, four. It doesn't matter. The fact that you went out with him, and apparently spent more than a few hours together, says a lot."

Kelly wanted to argue with her sister, but decided against it. Pamela Andrews-Porter refused to accept that she was exactly like their mother, Camille Andrews. She just could not resist meddling.

"I'm going to ring off because I have to go into town to do some shopping."

"Don't hang up yet, Kel. I was calling to let you know that Leo and I are hosting a Fourth of July cookout. Mama and Daddy are driving down for the weekend, and cousins Bill, Flora, Verna and her kids said they're coming up. It's going to be somewhat of a mini family reunion.''

"I'll be there.''

"Are you bringing your man?''

"No! And he's not my man.''

"You said that a little too quickly, little sis.''

"Goodbye, big sis.''

"Goodbye, Kelly,'' Pamela crooned, chuckling softly.

Kelly hung up, mumbling to herself. Just because she had slept with Ryan that did not mean he was her man or she his woman. What they had become were lovers before they'd become friends. How different it was from her relationship with Simeon. He had been her friend since first grade, and it wasn't until she was twenty that she offered him more than friendship: her body and a promise to love him forever.

She glanced at the clock on the table next to the phone. She had an hour to blow out her hair and ready herself for an afternoon of shopping with Ryan.

Ryan found his father by the pool. A few of the employees had gathered around the Olympic-size pool to cool off from the unseasonable ninety-degree temperatures. Two hundred feet away smaller bodies frolicked in the kiddie pool like baby seals under the watchful eyes of their parents.

Sitting down at the table under one of a dozen large black and red striped umbrellas positioned around the deck, he nodded at Sheldon. "Good afternoon."

Sheldon stared at his son through a pair of sunglasses. Missing was the tailored suit from the night before. This afternoon he wore jeans, T-shirt and a pair of running shoes.

"Good afternoon. How was your date?"

"Good."

He smiled, nodding. "How's Kelly?"

Ryan bit back a grin. "She's good."

Sheldon turned to stare out at the blue-green water. "I'm glad to hear it."

Ryan patted his father's bare shoulder. The sun had darkened his caffe latte complexion to skin to a rich cinnamon-brown. The muscle under his hand still hard for a middle-aged man in his prime.

"I like her, Pop." He inhaled a lungful of hot air. "I just hadn't realized how much l liked her until I was able to spend time with her. She has a quick mind and a wonderful sense of humor. She also has a sharp tongue."

Sheldon lifted his left eyebrow. "She sounds a lot like your mother."

Ryan chuckled. "It helps that she's beautiful and sexy."

Just like your mother was, Sheldon mused. "I'm glad you found someone you enjoy being with," he said aloud.

Gaze narrowing, Ryan searched the kiddie pool for his son. "Where's Sean?"

"He's in the dining hall eating lunch."

Ryan was pleased that Sean had begun eating again. During their stay in Alabama he'd refused to eat with the other children at the child care center. "I'm going to take him with me."

"Where are you going?"

"To Staunton. If Kelly's going to learn to ride, then she's going to need boots." Pushing to his feet, he said, "I'll see you later."

"Enjoy," Sheldon said in parting.

Sean sat between Ryan and Kelly in a specialty shop that featured leather goods, talking non-stop as she tried on several pairs of riding boots.

"Cook's gonna cook the three little pigs before the wolf eats them up." Kelly smiled at Ryan, who winked and returned her smile.

"Cook plans to roast a couple of pigs for the Memorial Day cookout, Sean, but I can assure you they are not *the* three little pigs," Ryan said in a quiet voice.

"Are you sure, Daddy?"

"Ask Miss Kelly."

She cut her eyes at Ryan who gave her a *please*

help me out expression. "Your father's right, Sean. When we go back to school on Monday—"

"Monday is no school, Miss Kelly," Sean interrupted. "You said it was Me—more Day."

She made a show of hitting her forehead with the heel of her hand. "That's right. I did forget that *Memorial* Day is Monday. Thank you for reminding me."

Sean patted Ryan's shoulder to get his attention. "We made flags in school."

"You didn't show it to me."

"You can't see it until Monday."

Sean explained to Ryan how they had counted the stars and stripes while Kelly indicated to the salesperson which pair of boots she had decided to purchase. Rising from his chair, Ryan reached into his rear pocket for a wallet, removed a credit card and handed it to the clerk.

Kelly reached for the card, but Ryan caught and held her wrist. "Let's not make a scene," he warned softly.

"There won't be a scene if you let me pay for my own purchases."

Curving an arm around her waist, he pulled her closer to his side. "What if we compromise?"

"How?"

"I pay for the boots and you pay for ice cream for the rest of the summer. It's going to work out equitably because Sean and I eat a lot of ice cream.''

Sean bobbed his head up and down. "That's right.''

Kelly knew when she was outnumbered. "How often do you eat it?''

"Every day," they choroused.

"I think I've just been had," she murmured under her breath.

They left the store and Ryan drove Sheldon's SUV to Shorty's Diner on Richmond Road. The restaurant looked like a 1950s jukebox. All stainless steel with neon lights and glass, it was colorful and inviting. Ryan ordered a monstrous ice-cream concoction large enough for four people.

Kelly, who rarely ate sweets, could not stop eating the homemade vanilla, strawberry and pistachio ice cream topped with nuts, whipped cream and fresh berries.

"You're going to make me fat," she whispered to Ryan as he helped her up into the SUV for the ride home.

"You'd look good with a few extra pounds."

"Not in the belly and butt," she growled.

"Especially in the belly," he countered, still holding the door open.

She went completely still, her gaze fusing with his. She berated herself for telling him she wanted a baby. And did she really want Ryan to father her child?

Was she ready for motherhood?

Did she want to marry again?

The questions taunted her because she had grown up believing one fell in love, married and then had children—in that order. She had done that with Simeon, but had not completed the cycle because he had been taken from her.

Turning to look out the windshield, she stared straight ahead. She had offered Ryan her body, but not her heart. She wasn't certain when she would— if ever.

Kelly met Ryan in the stables early Sunday morning. She found him kneeling in one of the stalls, examining the right foreleg of a stallion. A large black bag filled with rolls of bandages stood open on the floor.

She watched as he wrapped at least four layers of cotton wool and a bandage tightly around the leg. He removed a pair of latex gloves, dropping them in the bag and closing it.

"What happened to him?" she asked.

Ryan stood up, his gaze taking in everything about Kelly in one sweeping glance. Her hair was pulled back into a ponytail under a baseball cap. She was dressed for riding: blouse, jeans and boots. She held a pair of leather riding gloves in one hand.

"He sustained a simple fracture a couple of months ago."

"Will he be okay?"

He smiled. "He's healing nicely." Curving an arm around Kelly's waist, he led her to a door near the entrance. He punched several buttons on a panel, and the door opened automatically.

He ushered her into a large space where he had set up his office. It contained a large stainless-steel examining table, sinks, cabinets filled with bandages, vials of drugs, and surgical instruments.

"Do you perform surgeries here?"

He opened the bag, discarded the latex gloves, and then stored the bag on a corner shelf. "Only in an emergency. I'm a registered on-call vet with a hospital in Richmond."

He washed his hands in one of the sinks with a strong antiseptic-smelling solution, dried them on several paper towels, discarding the towels in a plastic-covered container.

Smiling at Kelly, he said, "Are you ready for your first riding lesson?"

She returned his smile. "Yes."

Taking her hand, he led her out of the stable to an area where Mark Charlesworth stood waiting with two saddled horses. Mark's expression brightened when he saw Kelly.

"Good morning, Miss Kelly."

"Good morning, Mark."

"Mark, please hold my horse while I help Miss Kelly."

Spanning her waist with both hands, Ryan swung her up effortlessly onto a horse. The horse side-stepped and he caught the reins, handing them to Kelly. "Hold them either in your right or left hand. Your fingers should close over the reins with your hand turned over so that the wrist is straight and your thumb up."

Kelly felt half a ton of muscle and raw power between her legs, refusing to acknowledge her fear as Ryan adjusted the stirrups to accommodate her legs. She'd never sat on a horse in her life, and the fact that she was at least six feet above the ground made her stomach roil.

"Put your feet in the stirrups, then lean forward in the saddle." She reacted like automaton once he showed her how to use her knees and reins to con-trol the animal.

The horse Ryan had chosen to ride reared up, his forelegs pawing the air. Mark tightened his hold on the bridle. "He's a little flighty this morning, Doc."

"That's because he wants to run." Ryan put his left foot in the stirrup, mounting in one continuous motion. Mark handed him his wide-brim hat. Reaching over, he held on to the bridle of Kelly's horse and he led her away from the stables.

Once she became accustomed to the rocking mo-tion, she found herself relaxing. She followed Ryan as he cantered toward the open portion of the property.

An hour later Kelly sat under a tree watching Ryan as he raced his horse across the verdant landscape. Horse and rider became one as the Thoroughbred established a long, low, raking stride. Sinking down to the grass, she closed her eyes.

Ryan returned to Kelly, finding her reclining on the grass, asleep. He tethered his horse next to where hers grazed on the sweet tender grass. He sank down beside Kelly, resting his head on his folded arm. She had taken off her cap. Without warning she opened her eyes.

"How do you like riding?"

"I like it, but I'm sore."

"Where?"

"My behind and between my legs."

Moving from his reclining position, he sat back on his heels. He did not give Kelly time to protest as he removed her boots. Her socks followed, then he unsnapped her jeans.

She slapped at his hand. "What are you doing?"

He pushed her hand away. "I'm going to give you a massage."

"No-ooo," she wailed in protest.

"Yes," he insisted, lifting her hips and easing her jeans down her legs. Any further protest ended once Ryan turned Kelly over to lie on her belly. "Rest your head on your arms."

She moaned once as gave herself up to the strength in his strong fingers as he kneaded her buttocks and the flesh of her inner thighs. After ten minutes he straddled her, his chest pressing against her back.

"You look as beautiful from behind as you do in front," he whispered against her ear.

Her breathing halted then started up again. "What are you doing?"

"It's not want I'm doing but what I want to do." Curving an arm around her middle, he eased her gently to her knees.

Kelly groaned inwardly when she felt the solid bulge in his groin pressing against her hips. The only shield between them was his jeans and her navy-blue thong panties.

Reaching between her legs, he cupped her feminine heat and desire shot through her like a jolt of electricity, leaving her wet and pulsing against his palm.

"Kelly," he growled deep in his throat.

"Now, Ryan," she gasped, praying she wouldn't climax before he penetrated her.

He unsnapped his jeans, pushing them and his briefs down around his knees and pulled aside the narrow strip of fabric. He entered her in one, swift, sure motion.

She felt his hot breath in her neck, raspy breathing in her ear, and the power in his thighs as he pushed into her pulsing flesh. Resting the back of her head on his shoulder, she closed her eyes, trying unsuccessfully not to explode.

Kelly had become a mare in heat as Ryan inhaled the feminine musk rising from between her legs. And like a rutting stallion, he gloried in the pleasure that came from pumping in and out of her lush body. Cupping his hands over her breasts he cradled them, measuring their weight as her nipples hardened under his fingertips.

He loved her, each deliberate thrust, joining their bodies, every gasp, groan, moan bringing them closer to the brink of a spiraling ecstasy and fulfillment. It was no longer flesh-to-flesh, man-to-woman, heart-to-heart, but soul-to-soul.

Pressing his face against the nape of her neck, Ryan caught the tender skin between his teeth, biting gently and leaving his brand. His lips left her neck and seared a path along the silken column of her neck.

Mouth open and gasping for her next breath, Kelly felt herself slipping away from reality. She writhed against Ryan, the curve of her buttocks tucked neatly against his groin. They had become a perfect fit.

Her body flamed and froze at the same time. Her world tilted and careened on its axis. She cried out for release and seconds later she exploded in a floodtide of shimmering fire that shattered the barrier she had erected around her heart to love again.

Kelly's passion spread to Ryan as her heat swept over him like a raging forest fire. His fingers tightened around her waist, holding her fast as he spewed liquid love into her still-pulsing flesh. He eased her down to the grass, gasping loudly.

Ryan pulled Kelly against his chest and buried his face in her hair. Everything that was Kelly Andrews seeped into his pores. He loved her!

He had fallen in love with her.

Easing back he stared at her staring back at him. In that instant he saw his unborn children in her eyes. The realization he had made to love to her without protection squeezed his heart. Splaying a hand over her hip, he kissed her moist forehead.

"I wanted to make love to you, but not without a condom."

She offered him a tender smile. "Don't beat up on yourself, Ryan. I'm safe right now."

"Are you certain?"

She nodded. "Yes. I woke up this morning with the familiar symptoms telling me I should see my period in a few days."

He wanted to tell her that it did not matter if she was or wasn't pregnant, because he loved her enough to ask her to share his love and his future.

They waited until their passions cooled and then

dressed. Ryan led Kelly to her horse, helped her mount before he mounted his. Their return to the stables was unhurried as they rode side by side in silence.

Ten

____

Ryan saw Kelly enter the dining hall, his gaze following her as she walked past his table and over to Mark Charlesworth's. The young stable hand rose to his feet at her approach. He went completely still when Mark cupped her elbow and led her away.

"Easy," Sheldon said softly, noting Ryan's thunderous expression. "It's not what you think."

Turning his head, Ryan stared at his father as if he were a stranger. "Just what is it I'm thinking, Pop?" The query, though spoken quietly, was ominous.

"There's nothing going on between them."

Ryan wanted to believe Sheldon. It was now the

end of June, and he and Kelly continued to see each other, but only on weekends. They had established a practice of sharing dinner, movie or concert, and a bed on Fridays at hotels far enough from Staunton to ensure their privacy.

He dropped off Sean and picked him up from school during the week. Kelly related to him the same way she related to the other parents. Knowing he was in love Kelly had increased Ryan's frustration because he wanted to spend more time with her. His need to spend more than twelve consecutive hours with her each week went beyond physical desire. One night they'd shared a bed but had been content to hold hands and talk rather than make love.

There was so much he longed to tell her but hesitated because she still withheld a small part of herself—the part that would allow her to love again. And there was nothing about Kelly that he did not love: her wit, intelligence, beauty, patience and her sensuality.

He planned to turn Blackstone Day School into a private school for grades N-6. He wanted to hire a music teacher so the children could learn to sing, read music and play musical instruments. The building would be expanded to include actual classrooms, and as the school's headmistress Kelly would hire and train the staff.

Ryan knew Kelly loved teaching as much as her

students loved her. Every day Sean came home singing her praises. He proudly displayed his art projects and showed Ryan his notebook filled with the letters of the alphabet and corresponding words for the letter of the day. Instead of playing with computer games or watching television, Sean now preferred reading picture books.

Kelly Andrews had become a positive role model for the children at Blackstone Farms, while at the same time she had taught the resident veterinarian that it was possible not to love once, but twice in a lifetime.

Floor lamps burned in the school's sitting area. Kelly sat with Mark, listening intently as he explained his answer to one of her questions. She had given him several practice PSAT examinations, and out of the possible sixteen hundred points, he averaged seven fifty-five on the math segment, but less than four hundred on the verbal.

Although his combined scores topped one thousand, she wanted him to increase his score on the verbal portion. It had taken two weeks for her to assess Mark's weak reading comprehension.

''You must train your eye to recognize key words within the paragraph. She circled half a dozen words with a pencil.

Mark studied the circled words. ''Is it B?''

Kelly shook her head. "You're guessing, Mark. Take your time."

He stared at the paragraph, exhaling audibly. "I can't, Miss Kelly."

"Yes, you can. If you can ace the math there's no reason why you can't ace the verbal as well."

He ran his hand over his dreaded hair. "Math has always been easy for me, but I've always had a problem with reading."

Kelly saw the frustration on his face. "Do you like reading?"

He shrugged a shoulder. "Not much."

"Do you read the newspaper?"

"No."

"Well, you should. There are three newspapers delivered to the farm—*USA Today, The Washington Post* and the *Virginian-Pilot.* I want you to read one every day. Underline the words you don't understand and look them up in the dictionary I gave you."

He grimaced. "Do I have to?"

Kelly wanted to laugh. He sounded so much like her younger students when they sought to get out of performing a task. "Yes, you do. I'm volunteering my time to help you, Mark. The least you can do is complete your homework assignments."

What Mark did not know was that she had sacrificed seeing Ryan during the week because she was committed to tutoring him. She wanted to see

Ryan more than just Friday nights. Waking up beside him on Saturday mornings in a strange hotel was not what she had envisioned for their relationship.

If she had been employed at the farm in any position other than a teacher, she would have eagerly dated Ryan openly. But she was his son's teacher, and for her this presented a personal conflict. She did not want Sean to know she had fallen in love with his father because she and Ryan talked about everything except a future together. He had not confessed to loving her, or she him.

And she was mature enough to know that falling in love with Ryan had nothing to do with sharing his bed. Ryan was intelligent, patient, generous and gentle despite his admission that he was once known as a brawler. He was a devoted father. He praised and encouraged Sean while setting limits for the child. Ryan took her to charming restaurants and even more charming hotels and inns for their overnight liaisons.

"I'll read the newspapers," Mark said, breaking into her musings.

She smiled at him. "Good. I'm going to make a list of vocabulary words for you to study. Come by tomorrow afternoon to pick it up."

Mark smiled, his deep-set dark eyes sparkling like polished onyx. "Thanks, Miss Kelly." Mark pushed his study manuals into a leather saddlebag, murmured a soft good night then turned and walked out of the schoolhouse.

The door closed and seconds later it opened again. Ryan stood in the doorway, staring at her. "Isn't he a little young for you?"

Kelly felt her pulse quicken. Could it be Ryan was jealous? And for him to display jealousy, then that meant his feelings went deeper than a mere liking?

"Yes, he is. So is your son. And don't forget the Smith twins."

Ryan didn't know whether to laugh in relief or kiss Kelly until she begged him to stop. It was apparent her relationship with Mark was that of teacher-student. He'd left the dining hall and was heading home when he saw the light coming from the schoolhouse. He'd told Sean to go back to Grandpa while he turned and walked to the school. He was less than twenty feet away when he saw Mark Charlesworth leaving. Maturity and his responsibility for Sean had stopped him when he thought about confronting Mark about Kelly. It was in that instant he knew he was still capable of brawling.

Walking over to wall-mounted bulletin board, he stared at the photographs and drawings depicting Blackstone Farms. "Exploring Our World" had become an enlightening experience for the five children who had lived on the farm since birth.

They'd taken photographs of the numbers tattooed under the upper lip of each horse that was used for identification purposes. They photographed Kevin Manning as he trained a horse, stable hands mucking out stalls, grooms brushing the hides of the horses to keep the coats free of eggs left by flies, men hauling bales of hay from the barn to the stables, more working to repair a fence to keep the horses from running away, and Carl Burton and his kitchen personnel.

His contribution was demonstrating preventive measures for keeping the horses healthy. They'd watched, transfixed, as he held a horse's mouth open and checked its teeth.

He read the penciled compositions of the children who wrote about the work their parents did at the horse farm. He smiled when he read: *My daddy is very strong, my mommy works hard.*

Kelly walked over to Ryan. "You were not supposed to see this until Parents' Night."

He stared at her under lowered lids. "And I'm not supposed to be alone with you until Friday."

She gasped. She had forgotten to tell Ryan. "I can't see you Friday."

"Why not?"

"I'm going to visit my sister in D.C. We're having a small family gathering for the Fourth of July holiday weekend."

Ryan's jaw tightened. The plans he had made to

take her and Sean to Williamsburg would have to be cancelled. "I wish you would've told me sooner."

"Why?"

"I'd planned to take you and Sean to Williamsburg for the weekend."

"You made plans without telling me?"

"I wanted it to be a surprise for you and Sean." He hadn't told anyone about the trip. Not even Sheldon.

"Well, it's more than a surprise. It's a shock."

"What's the problem, Kelly?" There was an edge to his voice she had never heard before.

She moved closer. "What signals are you sending to Sean when he sees his father and his teacher shack up together in a hotel room?"

Ryan struggled to contain his temper. "I reserved a suite with adjoining bedrooms. Sean and I would occupy one and you the other."

"Okay, so you have an answer for the sleeping arrangements. What about the three of us going away together? What are we telling Sean? That we're a couple and a family?"

His gray eyes bore into her. "We could be, Kelly."

She shook her head. "No, we can't, Ryan. Not without love. And if there's no love then you, me and Sean will never become a family."

The seconds ticked off in silence before Kelly

turned and walked out of the schoolhouse, leaving Ryan staring at where she had been. Reaching into the pocket of her jeans, she pulled out her keys. The lights were still on in the building when she drove away, tears blurring her vision.

She loved Ryan. Loved him so much it pained her to be in the same room with him. And she was realistic to know that he was drawn to her because of Sean. She'd confessed to wanting to become a mother, and he needed a mother for his son.

What was so ironic was that she and Ryan could both get wanted they wanted if only he told her that he loved her.

Kelly maneuvered her car into the winding driveway to her sister's home, parking behind a late-model sedan bearing New York plates. Her parents had arrived before she had.

She retrieved a bag from the trunk, leaving it open, then made her way up the steps to the wraparound porch. The inner door stood open, and she peered through the screen door. She tried the door, finding it locked. Ringing the bell, she waited for someone to answer it.

A smile crinkled the skin around her eyes she spied her brother-in-law striding toward her with a coal-black ball of fur at his heels. "Hey, Leo."

He unlocked the door and held it open. "Hey, yourself." He kissed her cheek. "You look good,

Kelly." He sniffed her neck. "And you smell nice for someone hanging out with horses."

She returned the kiss, his neatly barbered beard grazing her lips. "Not only am I hanging with horses, but I'm learning to ride."

"I'd willingly bet a week's salary to see you clinging to the back of a horse."

"Hold on to your wallet, because you'll lose. I sit a horse, not cling to it."

"Uhuh," he teased. "Let me take your bag up to your room."

Kelly tightened her grip on the leather handles. "I can carry it. You can get the carton in my car. I left the trunk open."

Tall, handsome and with a smooth-shaven head, Leo Porter wagged a finger. "You know you're not supposed to bring anything." Because of their careers and active social life the Porters had made it a practice to cater their parties.

"Oh, well," she crooned. "Then I'll just take the wine back to Blackstone Farms with me."

Leo hugged her. "Where did you find it?"

"In a quaint little store not too far from Lexington." Kelly smiled down at the puppy licking her toes. "Who is this?"

"That's Miss Porter. Pam and I call her Poe-Poe. We got her a week ago."

"Is she paper trained?"

"Yes. Pam wouldn't have a dog in her house unless it was trained."

Bending, Kelly scooped the puppy up. "Hello, Miss Porter." The poodle pup yipped and wiggled. "Okay, I'll put you down." She placed the dog on the floor and she took off, her feet slipping out from under her on the highly waxed wood floor. She rolled several feet before regaining her footing.

"I'll meet you in the back," Kelly said as she walked through the entryway of the spacious Colonial.

It took less than fifteen minutes to unpack, wash her face and brush her hair. As she secured it in a ponytail, she made a mental note to call the salon she had visited when living in D.C. to make an appointment.

She skipped down the carpeted staircase and made her way through the modern kitchen to a door leading to the Porters' expansive backyard.

Camille sat on a chair, her silver-haired head covered by a wide straw hat, laughing at something her first cousin had said to her. Her clear-brown eyes widened as she spied Kelly. Holding out her arms, she stood up.

Kelly walked over to her mother and sank into her comforting embrace. "Hi, Mama."

Pulling back and holding Kelly at arm's length, Camille nodded. "You look wonderful Kelly. Look at your baby, Horace," she called to her husband who was engrossed in a chess game.

Pushing back his chair, he pointed a finger at his brother-in-law. "Don't you breathe until I get back," he warned. Turning, Horace Andrews turned the brilliance of his smile on his youngest daughter.

"Hello, Daddy," Kelly said before she kissed his rounded cheek. Resting a hand over his belly, she whispered, "You need to go on a diet."

Horace grimaced. "Not only do you look like your mother, but now you're beginning to sound like her."

"But you're sixty, Daddy—"

"I happen to know how old I am," he countered, cutting her off. "Your mother haunts and nags me constantly about losing weight. And I will."

"When, Daddy?"

"When I get to be a *grandfather*," he countered with a wide grin.

"Stop it, Daddy! You and Mama have to stop this insanity about becoming grandparents or it will never happen."

"Pamela and Leo would rather get a *dog* than have a baby." He'd spat out the word.

"That's their choice and their business." She had enunciated each word. Horace Andrews mumbled under his breath about what his children could do with their choices. Patting his arm, she said softly,

"Go back to your game. I want to speak to Cousin Flora."

Pamela lay on the pillow next to Kelly the way they'd done when they were growing up together. "How are you and your Blackstone?"

Turning on the side and facing Pamela, Kelly rested her head on her folded arm. People would never take her and Pamela for sisters, because they looked nothing alike. Her older sister was the image of their paternal grandmother: petite, delicate features, black curly hair and sable coloring.

"His name is Ryan. We're doing all right."

"Just all right?"

Kelly lifted her left shoulder. "We see each other on Fridays and spend the night together. We usually get back to the farm before noon on Saturday."

Pamela's waxed eyebrows wrinkled. "You're sleeping together off the property?"

"He has a four-year-old son who just happens to be my student."

Pamela mouth formed a perfect *O*. "I see where you're coming from." She gave Kelly a long, penetrating stare. "You're in love with him, aren't you?"

"Am I that transparent?"

"No. It's just that you seem so calm—at peace with yourself."

Kelly wanted to tell Pamela she was wrong.

What she was feeling wasn't serenity, but turmoil. She wanted to tell Ryan that she loved him, but balked each time she lay in his arms. And she did love him enough to marry him and bear his children. All he had to do was open his mouth and ask her.

Eleven

Ryan's hand flailed out as he tried brushing away whatever it was crawling over his cheek. He moaned and turned over onto his belly. Seconds later a sliver of ice trickled down his spine and he sprang off the bed, his hands bunched into fists, but was rendered immobile by an arm around his throat, cutting off his breath.

"You still have good reflexes for an old man," a familiar voice whispered in his ear.

"Dammit, Jeremy!"

Jeremy Blackstone released Ryan's throat and stepped back quickly as his older brother swung at him. Grinning, he winked. He had anticipated his reaction.

Ryan stood in the middle of his bedroom, muscular arms crossed over his bare chest. It had been more than a year since he'd seen Jeremy. He didn't look any older, but there was something about him that communicated danger. As an undercover agent for the Drug Enforcement Administration it was obvious that he had become as hardened and dangerous as the criminals he sought to bring to justice.

"How did you get in?" He was certain he had locked the door before he retired for the night.

Jeremy lifted a thick black eyebrow. "I picked the lock."

"You're nothing more than a legal thug."

"You should try it. Thug life ain't too bad."

"No thanks. Do you mind if I put some clothes on?"

Shrugging his broad shoulders, Jeremy moved over and sat in an armchair. "It doesn't bother me what you wear. You happen not to be my type."

Crossing the bedroom, Ryan opened a drawer and took out a pair of boxers. He slipped into them and walked over and sat down on a matching chair opposite his brother. Jeremy's pitch-black hair was longer than he had seen it in years. Pulled back off his forehead and secured in a ponytail on his nape, the style provided an unfettered view of his striking olive-brown face with a pair of high cheekbones, aquiline nose, firm mouth, short dark beard and dove-gray eyes. Diamond studs glittered in each ear.

Ryan knew Jeremy had had his ears pierced when on an undercover assignment in South America, but this was the first time he could recall him wearing earrings at Blackstone Farms.

"How long are you staying?"

"I'm out of here tomorrow night."

"That only gives you one day. Why do you bother to come if you can't stay for more than a day?"

Jeremy frowned. "Now, you sound like Pop."

"That's because he's right, Jeremy. Once you become a father you'll understand how he feels when he doesn't hear from you for months. And he has no way of knowing whether you're dead or alive."

"That's because he refuses to accept what I've chosen to do with my life."

"He doesn't have to accept your career. All he has to do is accept you as his son. A son he loves, a son he worries about. And maybe even a son who may one day claim his rightful place at Blackstone Farms."

Jeremy leaned over, resting his elbows on his knees. "Read my lips, Ryan. I don't do horses. I don't know what has Pop all bent out of shape. You're a brilliant veterinarian rumored to be able to raise horses from the dead."

Ryan's eyebrows lowered as he glared at Jeremy. "This is not a joke." Jeremy sobered quickly. "I might know horses, but you're the one with the business background. Pop has been running this farm for a long time, and even though he's not complaining I know he's tired. Before I left to teach at Tuskegee I picked up some the slack, but since I've been back I realize that it takes more than one person to run a farm this size."

Jeremy swore under his breath. "Please don't pressure me, Ryan. I'm not ready to stop doing what I'm doing."

"I'm not asking you to stop. I'm just asking you to consider your options."

"Okay. I'll think about it."

"Good." Ryan stood up and extended his hand. He wasn't disappointed when Jeremy grasped it. "Why don't you bed down in the room next to Sean's?"

Jeremy shook his head. "I'd rather sleep in my own place."

"It hasn't been aired out."

"That's all right." He stood up, stretching his six-foot-three height. "I've slept in worse conditions." And he had. "If I'm not up by eight, then come and get me. Other than missing you, Pop and Sean, the thing I miss the most is Cook's pancakes."

"Okay." Ryan glanced at the clock on his bedside table. It was a few minutes past four. It was too early to get up, but he knew he wouldn't be able to go back to sleep.

Walking over to the window, he peered out through the screen. The odor of spent fireworks lingered in the early-morning air. Sheldon had hired a professional fireworks company to put on a dazzling display of brilliant color for the children who lay on blankets with their parents, staring up at the sky while cheering and applauding each explosion. Sean kept asking him whether Miss Kelly could see the color from where she was. Ryan told him he didn't believe she could, but his son mentioning her name made their separation even more acute.

Turning on his heel, he made his way into an adjoining bathroom to shave and shower.

Kelly felt as if she had truly come home once she crossed the property line leading to Blackstone Farms. She spied the flagpole with the American flag flying atop the black and red one that represented the farm's silks. The flags hung limply in the falling rain.

She had had a fun-filled relaxing weekend with her family. She went to bed late, slept in even later and generally did not do anything more strenuous than shift a lounger to a shaded area whenever the sun burned her exposed skin.

Sighing audibly, Kelly maneuvered under the

carport beside her bungalow. Recurring thunder-storms with torrential downpours had slowed her return trip. She switched off the wipers, lights and the engine. Pushing open the door, she inhaled the smell of wet earth.

Walking the short distance to the porch, she mounted the stairs. She caught movement out of the corner of her eye and froze. Rising from the love seat in the shadows was the outline of a man. The scent of a familiar cologne wafted in her nostrils. It was Ryan. He had waited for her to come home.

"Ryan?"

"Yes, princess."

"What are you doing here?" He hadn't moved out of the shadows.

"I was waiting to welcome you back to *our* home."

"This is *your* home, Ryan."

"It could be yours if you want it to be."

Her breath caught in her lungs. What did he mean? What was he trying to tell her? Shifting, she tried making out his expression but failed. It was too dark.

"I don't understand."

"What is there to understand?" he asked instead of answering her question. He took two long strides, bringing him inches from her. "I want you to stay here—forever."

She shook her head. "That's not possible, Ryan."

His hand touched the side of her face. The smell of his cologne mingled with that of his laundered shirt. "Yes, it is, princess. It's possible if you marry me."

She couldn't move or speak. The word she longed to tell him was lodged in the back of her throat, refusing to come out. She wanted so much to tell him yes; yes she would marry him; yes she would become the mother Sean never had; yes she would be honored to have his babies. She would say yes to everything, but not without his declaration of love.

"I can't," she whispered instead.

"Is he still in your heart?" Ryan snapped. "Is a dead man still standing between us? I'm not asking you to forget Simeon, darling." His voice was softer, calm. "All I want is for you to let me in."

"You're in, Ryan. How I feel about you has nothing to do with Simeon."

"Then what is it?"

Looping her arms around his waist, she laid her head against his chest, and listened the strong pumping of his heart under her ear. "Love."

"Love?" he repeated.

"Yes."

"You think I don't love you?"

"I don't know what to think, Ryan, because you've never told me that you loved me."

He swung her up in his arms. "Of course I love you, Kelly. Do you think I would ask you to marry me if I didn't love you?"

She buried her face against his warm throat. "I was waiting for you to tell me you loved me before I told you how I felt about you."

"Well, I'm waiting."

Tightening her hold around his neck, she pressed her mouth to his. "I love you, Ryan Blackstone."

His smile was dazzling. "Thank you, my darling. Now, isn't there something else you want to say to me?"

"Nope," she said sassily.

"Give me your keys, Kelly."

"What's the magic word?"

"Please." The word was forced out between his teeth.

She placed her keys in his outstretched palm, holding onto his neck while he unlocked the door. Shifting her body, he flipped a wall switch, turning on the table lamp in the parlor. Ryan looked at Kelly, his eyes widening in surprise. She had cut her hair. Soft curls were brushed off her forehead and over her ears.

"You look incredible."

A blush burned her cheeks. "Thank you."

He dropped a kiss on the top of her head. "You're welcome."

She met his gaze, smiling. The love she saw radiating from the sooty orbs made her want to cry. He loved her! He loved her and she loved him.

Kelly closed her eyes and inhaled deeply. "Yes, Ryan. Yes, I will marry you and become mother to *our* children."

Ryan carried her across the parlor and he walked into Kelly's bedroom for the first time. The time for hiding his love for her ended the moment she'd accepted his marriage proposal.

He had loved and lost and so had she, but it was time for new beginnings. He knew he could not replace the memory of her first husband and did not want to. What they would create would be new memories to reminiscence about whenever they watched a future generation of Blackstones lie on the grass and gasp in awe at Fourth of July fireworks.

Bending slightly, he lowered Kelly until her feet touched the coolness of the wood floor. She walked over to a bedside table and turned on a lamp. The space was flooded with soft golden light that illuminated an exquisite sleigh bed and towering armoire. The soft colors of lemon yellow and lime-green were predominant. The bedroom was romantic and feminine—just like the woman he had fallen in love with.

"It ends tonight, princess. No more making love in hideaway places. No more pretending that my only contact with you is because you're Sean's teacher."

Raising her hand, Kelly beckoned Ryan closer. She stared up at him as he walked over to her. She placed her hands in the middle of his chest. "I want this night to be special, so special that I will remember it for the rest of my life."

Ryan wanted to tell her that what was to occur between them would be only one of many more special nights to come. There would be their wedding night, the night they'd celebrate their first wedding anniversary, the tenth, twentieth, thirtieth, fiftieth, the birth of their first child and the others he hoped they would have.

His hands covered her back, burning her flesh through her cotton blouse. Pulling her closer, he lowered his head and tasted her mouth. Her lips parted and his tongue mated with hers, plunging and pulling back, as he simulated making love to her.

Kelly writhed against Ryan in an attempt to get even closer. It had taken only three days away from him to make her crave him. How had she existed every Sunday through Thursday not having him touch her?

His hands moved lower, cupping her hips and allowing her to feel the solid bulge in his jeans. His hardness electrified her as she moaned and exhaled into his open mouth.

Ryan forced himself to go slow. He wanted to prolong their coming together as long as possible. He caught the tip of her tongue between his teeth and sucked gently while pulling it into his mouth. Kelly moaned in protest, but he refused to let her go. He sucked a little harder and suddenly she went pliant in his arms. He had to release her tongue when he swept her up in his arms and placed her on the bed.

Moving over her body, his lips seared a hot path down her neck and under her ears. His hands went to the buttons on her blouse. Suddenly fingers that were trained to perform the most delicate surgical procedures were heavy and clumsy. Placing both hands at the neckline, he pulled at the fabric. It parted, buttons flying in every direction.

The sight of her dark nipples showing through the sheer fabric of her white bra was his undoing. Ryan did not remember undressing Kelly or himself. What he did remember was sliding down the length of her body and drinking deeply from between her legs. He remembered turning her over and running his tongue down the length of her spine and over the curve of her hips. He remembered tasting and sampling every inch of her fragrant body as her moans of pleasure echoed his labored breathing.

It was when he guided his swollen flesh into her hot, wet pulsing flesh that he forgot everything. Slipping his hands under her hips, he held her as he pushed into her again and again.

Kelly gloried in the hard body atop hers. Her breasts tingled against his hair-roughened chest, whenever she arched to meet his downward thrusts. She trailed her fingernails up and down Ryan's back, eliciting deep groans from him. Without warning, he reversed position. She almost toppled off the bed with the sudden motion, but he caught her around the waist, holding her protectively.

A smile curved her mouth. He knew it was a position she favored because it allowed for deeper penetration and for her to set the pace for their coming together. Leaning back, she closed her eyes and established a slow rocking motion that mimicked her riding a horse. Ryan's hardness touched the walls of her womb, and she screamed out her climax, shaking uncontrollably as her screams became soft moans of satisfaction. Spent, she collapsed to his damp chest.

The muscles in Ryan's neck strained; he struggled not to pour out his passions into her hot body. Waves of ecstasy throbbed through him like blood rushing through veins, carrying precious oxygen to the heart. He tried holding back but the rush of desire seized him and sent him hurtling into a dimension where he experienced free-fall for the first time in his life.

They lay together, still joined, and waited until their respiration slowed enough for them to breathe without gasping. Their coming together was special; the night was special.

Kelly moved, shifting until her legs were sandwiched between Ryan's. The odor of their lovemaking blended with the perfume and cologne on their bodies. Resting her check on his breastbone, she sighed softly, knowing she would never forget a single detail of this joining.

Ryan ran his fingers through her short hair. "When do you want marry, darling?"

Raising her head, she met his gaze. "How about a month from now?"

"You want to wait that long?"

"That's not long, Ryan."

"For me it is."

"Aren't you forgetting about Sean?"

Ryan's forehead furrowed. "What about him?"

"He needs time to get used to me sharing his father with him."

"Sean is crazy about you."

"That may be true, but we'll still need a period of adjustment. Right now he sees me as his teacher, not his mother."

"What do you want him to call you?"

"That will be up to him."

Holding hands, they planned their upcoming nuptials. Kelly told Ryan she wanted to be married at Blackstone Farms. She expressed a desire have her sister as her matron of honor, while Ryan said he would ask Sheldon to stand in as his best man.

"I have someone I want you to meet," he said cryptically.

"Who?"

"My brother."

Kelly sat up. "He's here now?"

Ryan nodded. "He's leaving tomorrow night."

She wanted to meet the other Blackstone son— the one who had partnered Ryan during their adolescent mishaps. "Is it possible to meet him now, because I've made plans to take the children into town for a puppet show tomorrow."

Sitting up, Ryan swung his legs over the side of the bed. "Sure."

Kelly moved off the bed, smiling. "Race you to the shower." She hadn't taken more than two steps when Ryan caught her around her waist, swept her off her feet and carried her over his shoulder into the bathroom.

Kelly felt a shiver of apprehension as she walked up the porch steps to Sheldon's home. It was only the second time she had entered the spacious structure. The first time had been for her interview.

What had caught her attention during that visit

was a quartet of curio cabinets filled with trophies, mementoes and faded photographs of black jockeys dating back to the mid-nineteenth century. Sheldon had proudly revealed that of the fifteen jockeys at the first Kentucky Derby at Churchill Downs in Louisiana in 1875, fourteen were black. Oliver Lewis, riding Aristides, became the first black to win the Derby. However, it was Isaac Murphy who was considered to be one of the greatest jockeys in U.S. racing history.

She followed Ryan through a formal dining room into a smaller room where she had sat while Sheldon had questioned her about her credentials and experience.

Her gaze met and fused with a pair of gray eyes that reminded her of Sheldon and Ryan's. Whereas Ryan's eyes reminded her of lightning, Jeremy's made her think of a cloaking fog. He stood up, his gaze narrowing. Seconds later, Sheldon also stood up.

Ryan curved an arm around Kelly's waist, the action communicating protection and possession. The gesture was not lost on Sheldon.

"Ah, Miss Kelly."

She nodded. "Good evening, Sheldon."

A mysterious smile curved Ryan's mouth. "Jeremy, this is Miss Kelly Andrews, my fiancée." He ignored his father's gasp. "Kelly, my brother and former partner in crime, Jeremy."

"When...when did you two decide this?" Sheldon sputtered.

Jeremy leaned over and kissed Kelly's cheek. "Welcome to the family. Don't say I didn't warn you, but you're about to have the ride of your life," he added, whispering in her ear.

She smiled at Jeremy, deciding she liked him. There was no doubt he and Ryan were brothers because they looked so much alike. But that's where the similarity ended. There was something about Jeremy that was overtly dangerous. A sixth sense told her he was a magnet for trouble.

Sheldon pursed his lips, whistling loudly. Everyone went completely still. Three pairs of eyes were fixed on him. "Will someone please tell me if there's going to be a wedding?"

Ryan smiled. "Yes, Pop, there's going to be a wedding. Kelly and I plan to marry sometime next month."

Sheldon crossed his arms over his chest in a gesture Kelly had seen Ryan affect so many times. "I'll say it again. When did you decide this?"

"Tonight," Kelly said in a quiet voice.

Sheldon's expression was impassive. "Are you sure you want to marry my son and spend the rest of your life on a horse farm?"

"Pop!" Ryan's voice bounced off the walls.

Kelly caught his arm, feeling tension tightening the muscles. "It's all right, darling." Jeremy and

Sheldon exchanged glances at the endearment. Giving Sheldon a direct stare, she said, "The answer is yes to both questions. I will marry Ryan, and I plan to spend the rest of my life living on a horse farm raising our children to love this land and honor the heritage left them by their ancestors."

"Boo-yaw!" Sheldon yelled, pumping his fist in the air.

Ryan and Jeremy howled, slapping each other's back while shouting, "Boo-yaw!"

"This calls for a celebratory drink," Sheldon said as he made his way over to a liquor cabinet. He took out a bottle of aged bourbon. "I've been saving this for a long time. The last time this old girl and I danced together was the day I became a grandfather." He gave Kelly a level stare. "You are able to imbibe, aren't you?"

At first she did not understand his question, but realization dawned. He probably thought the reason she and Ryan had planned to marry so quickly was because she was pregnant.

"Yes, I am."

"Daddy? Are you having a party?"

Everyone turned to find Sean standing in the doorway, rubbing his eyes. He was dressed in a pair of lightweight cotton pajamas. It was apparent the loud voices had awakened him.

Ryan smiled at Sean. "Yes. Come in." Sean padded barefoot into the den, and found himself cradled in his father's arms. "We're celebrating because Miss Kelly and I are going to be married."

Sean's eyes widened with this disclosure. "She…she's going to be my mama?"

Pressing a kiss to his son's forehead, Ryan said, "Yes, she is."

His eyes sparkled. "She's going to be my mama and my teacher?"

Ryan nodded. "Yes."

Pumping his fist like he'd seen his grandfather do, he crowed, "Boo-yaw!"

Kelly doubled over in laughter, unable to stop until tears rolled down her cheeks. Jeremy was right. She was in for a wild ride—one she looked forward to taking over and over again.

Twelve

Sheldon and Jeremy raised snifters filled with an ounce of premium bourbon and toasted Ryan and Kelly. Sean, standing between his grandfather and uncle, lifted his glass of apple juice.

"To Daddy and my new Mama," he said, giggling.

Kelly felt her eyes fill. Blinking, she smiled through her tears. "Thank you, Sean." She touched her glass to Sean's, Ryan's, Jeremy's and finally Sheldon's. She took a sip, holding the liquor in her mouth for several seconds before letting it slide down the back of her throat. It detonated on impact.

"Whoa!" she gasped.

Sheldon nodded his approval. "See why this old girl only comes to the dance every few years?"

Jeremy also gasped, holding his throat. "Boo-ahhh!" he whispered.

"Ditto," Ryan added after swallowing. He placed his glass on a sideboard. "That's enough of that."

Reaching for the bottle, Jeremy studied the label. "I've never heard of this brand. Pop, are you certain this stuff isn't moonshine?"

Sheldon shook his head. "I never thought my boys would grow up to be such sissies." He drained his glass, reached for Sean, and swung him up in his arms. Cradling his grandson's head to his shoulder, he whispered loudly, "It's time for the men of the house to turn in for the night." He blew a kiss at Kelly as he strode out of the room.

Jeremy walked over to Kelly and hugged her. "Congratulations again. I'm with Pop and Sean. I'm going to bed." He patted Ryan's shoulder. "All the best, brother."

Waiting until they were alone, Ryan curved his arms around Kelly's waist. "I want you to come back to my place with me. I'd like to show you something."

"What?"

He flashed a mysterious smile. "You'll see."

Kelly found herself in the middle of the living room of a house that was soon to become her home.

The two-story, three-bedroom structure was the equivalent of one city block away from the ones occupied by Sheldon and Jeremy. Ryan had informed her that his father had first taken up residence in the house after he'd returned from a tour of duty in Vietnam.

The furnishings were formal and elegant. Every chair, table and lamp was meticulously positioned as if for a magazine layout. It was perfect, a little too perfect. A slight frown appeared between her eyes. There was something wrong with the room. Suddenly it hit her! It didn't look lived in. Staring at a sofa and matching love seat, Kelly mentally catalogued what she would rearrange. Firstly she would take down the drapes and replace them with a lighter weight fabric to let in the natural light.

Walking over the fireplace, she studied the framed photographs lining the mantel. Smiling, she recognized a younger Sheldon in a United States Army uniform with his young smiling bride. Peering closely at the picture, she noted Julia Blackstone's natural beauty. Ryan had inherited her smile.

There were photographs of Ryan and Jeremy as children, and more of Sean at different ages. Nowhere was there a photograph of Sean's mother. It was if she'd been completely erased from his life. She heard footfalls, and turned around. Ryan had returned, holding a small wooden box.

He cupped her elbow, leading her over to sit on the sofa. He placed the box on her lap. "Open it."

She sprang a latch, the lid opening. Staring back at her on a bed of black velvet was a solitaire ring with a large square-cut blue-white diamond; along with the ring was a pair of drop South Sea pearl earrings dangling from a diamond cluster, and a bangle of diamond baguettes.

"They are beautiful, Ryan."

"They belonged to my great grandmother. My mother gave them to me a month before she died. She wanted me to give them to my wife."

She gave him an incredulous look. "Why didn't you give them to Sean's mother?"

His expression was impassive. "I'd offered them to her, but she said she didn't want someone else's hand-me-downs. The pieces in that box were purchased from Cartier between 1917 and 1919."

She picked up the bangle. "It's heavy."

"That's because all of the pieces are set in platinum."

"What about Jeremy?"

"Don't worry, princess. Jeremy was given his share."

Reaching around her, Ryan picked up the box with the jewelry. He took the ring and slipped it on the third finger of Kelly's left hand. It was a perfect fit.

She extended her hand. The light from a floor

lamp caught the diamond, prisms of light catching and radiating from the flawless gem.

Ryan curved an arm around Kelly's shoulders when she rested her head on his shoulder. "We're going to have to choose a date."

"What about the last weekend in August."

"How about the first weekend?" he countered.

Easing back, she stared at him. "That's only three weeks away."

"I know. We can go up to Saratoga Springs, New York before the summer racing season ends. I know it's not much of a honeymoon, but I'd like to take you away, even if it's only for a weekend. We can take a real honeymoon during the Christmas break."

"How long is the racing season?"

"Six weeks."

Kelly wondered if she could pull everything together in three weeks. She had to send out invitations, get a dress and select a ring for Ryan.

"Okay," she agreed, kissing his cheek. "I'm going back to D.C. at the end of the week to get my sister to help me with invitations. And while I'm there I'll do some shopping."

Ryan pulled her across his lap. "If you need help with anything, just let me know."

She nuzzled his neck, breathing a kiss under his ear. "You need to take me back to my place."

"Why?" he crooned.

"Because I have to go to sleep, Ryan. I'm going need all of my energy for my students tomorrow."

"Sleep here tonight."

"No. Not until we're married."

Pulling back he stared at her. "Don't tell me I'm marrying an old-fashioned girl?"

"I'm more conservative than old-fashioned. That comes from working with young children. After all, they learn from example."

Kelly had no way of knowing that when she answered an ad for a teaching position on a horse farm she would find a love that promised forever.

Kelly slept restlessly throughout the night, and when she left her bed at six she felt as if she had been up all night. She brewed a small carafe of coffee, drank several cups, then dialed the area code for D.C.

Pamela answered the phone with a cheery, "Good morning."

"Pamela, this is Kelly."

There came a pause. "What's with the Pamela?"

"I have good news to tell you."

"When are you due?"

"I'm not pregnant!" she practically shouted. Well, she didn't think she was pregnant. When she and Ryan had made love the night before he hadn't used a condom. Squinting she calculated when she'd last had her period. Sighing, she realized she was safe.

"I'm getting married in three weeks here at the farm, and I'm going to need your help with addressing invitations and shopping for a dress."

Pamela screamed at the top of her lungs, eliciting a frantic barking from Miss Porter. "I can't believe it," she said over and over. A loud sniffle came through the earpiece. "Dang, Kel. I can't believe I'm crying and souping snot at the same time. Wait until I blow my nose."

"Pamela?" Kelly said into the receiver when a full minute elapsed without her sister coming back to the phone.

"I'm back. I had to tell Leo the good news."

"I'm coming in this weekend."

"Is there anything you want me to do on this end in the meantime?

"Yes. I need you to use your artistic talents and design an invitation for me. I have to get Ryan's full name and the directions to Blackstone Farms. And you and I have to do some serious shopping in Chevy Chase."

"Where are you going?"

"Ryan and I are going up to Saratoga Springs next month for a weekend."

"Now, Miss Clotheshorse, you're singing my song."

Kelly laughed. She and Pamela had gotten their

love of shopping from their mother. For Camille it was hats, Pamela handbags and Kelly's weakness was shoes.

"I'm going to call Mama and give her the news as soon as I hang up with you."

"Kel?"

"Yes, Pam."

"I'm so happy for you."

"Thanks, big sis."

She rang off and dialed her mother's number. The call lasted less than five minutes, and when she hung up it was Kelly's turn to shed tears of joy.

A portable stage had been set up under a tent large enough to accommodate the sixty invited guests and more than thirty of Blackstone Farms' extended family. It had rained steadily for two days, then the night before Ryan Blackstone was scheduled to exchange vows with Kelly Andrews, but after the rain had stopped, a strong wind swept the clouds across the sky to reveal an orange-yellow near-full moon.

Kelly stood beside Ryan, eyes closed, repeating her vows. She was afraid that if she looked at him she wouldn't be able to hold back her tears. Her hands were trembling as she slipped a platinum and yellow gold band on Ryan's finger.

She heard the judge telling Ryan he could kiss his bride, and her world stood still as she felt the pressure of his firm lips on hers, sealing their troth. It was over. She was now Mrs. Ryan Jackson Blackstone.

Ryan pulled Kelly closer, her soft curves melding with the hardness of his body. He'd run the race and won the ultimate prize.

"Didn't I warn you, Mrs. Blackstone?"

"About what?" she whispered against his warm mouth.

"That I play for keeps."

Her smile was as dazzling as the sun warming the earth. "So, do I, Mr. Blackstone."

Turning they faced all of the people who had come to witness another generation of Blackstones solidifying their place in Virginia's horse country's history.

Epilogue

Four months later…

Ryan sat at the desk in his office when the door opened. Glancing up he saw Mark Charlesworth holding a large vase with a bouquet of flowers wrapped in pale pink cellophane.

"These came for you, Doc."

Rising to his feet, Ryan smiled. "Who sent them?"

"Me." Kelly moved into the doorway, grinning at her husband.

Mark placed the flowers on a table and winked at Kelly as he walked out of the vet's office. Miss

Kelly had asked him to carry the vase to Dr. Blackstone, because she did not want to lift anything that was too heavy. The glow in her eyes and her mysterious smile meant that the resident veterinarian was going to receive wonderful news.

Mark had received a bouquet of flowers from Miss Kelly once he received his test results from his college entrance exam. He had received a combined score of thirteen hundred sixty on the SAT. He was going to college! He would miss Blackstone Farms, but knew he would come back one day—as a veterinarian.

Kelly watched Ryan watching her. "Congratulations, Dr. Blackstone."

He moved closer, his gaze fixed on her moist lips. "For what, Mrs. Blackstone."

Reaching for his left hand, she placed it over her flat belly. "For this."

His gaze widened until she saw their black depths. "Are you sure?"

Her lids lowered. "As sure as I am that I'll love you forever."

Gathering Kelly to his chest, he picked her up and swung her around and around until she pleaded with him to stop.

Throwing back his head, he shouted, "Boo-yaw!"

Caught up in his infectious joy, Kelly whispered close to his ear, ''Boo-yaw to you, too.''

''Now I know you can do better than that with the Blackstone cheer.''

Rising her chin, she closed her eyes and shouted ''Boo-yaw!''

Ryan lowered his head and kissed her long and deep. They were still locked in a passionate embrace when some of the stable hands came to see what the shouting was all about.

Three men crowded in the doorway to find their boss cradling his wife to his chest. Their gazes shifted to the flowers and they backed away, smiling.

''Something tells me that we're going to have another celebration soon,'' one said quietly.

And Blackstone Farms had a lot to celebrate. Their jockeys had stood within the chalk markings of the winner's circle in the last five of the six races they had run.

But the best celebration was still to come—with the birth of another Blackstone come summer.

* * * * *

New York Times **Bestselling Author**

JAYNE ANN KRENTZ

writing as Stephanie James

Dangerous Affair

Sizzling emotion and
compelling characters in
two classic novels about
two women who've fallen
for the wrong man!

Jayne Ann Krentz is
"one of the hottest writers
in romance today."
—*USA TODAY*

Look for it—March 2004.

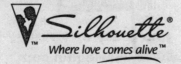

Silhouette® Desire®

Looking for the mystery man at Mar Brisas Resort for another trip to heaven. Let's meet on the endless white sand for more pleasure in paradise. You can find it at Mar Brisas….
—The Lady in Blue

Nicole Whitaker had designed the billboard ad to bring in business to her dying hotel. But when her mystery man answers the ad, she gets a whole lot more than she bargained for!

Don't miss

Like a Hurricane
(Silhouette Desire #1572)

by

ROXANNE
ST. CLAIRE

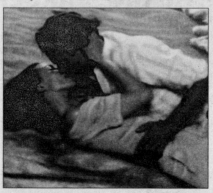

Available March 2004 at your favorite retail outlet.

The captivating family saga of the Danforths continues with

Sin City Wedding
by
KATHERINE GARBERA
(Silhouette Desire #1567)

When ex-flame Larissa Nelson showed up on Jacob Danforth's doorstep with a child she claimed was his, the duty-bound billionaire demanded they marry. A quickie wedding in Vegas joined Jacob and the shy librarian in a marriage of convenience...but living as husband and wife stirred passions that neither could deny—nor resist.

DYNASTIES : THE DANFORTHS

A family of prominence...
tested by scandal, sustained by passion!

Available March 2004 at your favorite retail outlet.

COMING NEXT MONTH

#1567 SIN CITY WEDDING—Katherine Garbera
Dynasties: The Danforths
When ex-flame Larissa Nelson showed up on Jacob Danforth's doorstep with a child she claimed was his, the duty-bound billionaire demanded they marry. A quickie wedding in Vegas joined Jacob and the shy librarian in a marriage of convenience, but living as husband and wife stirred passions that neither could deny…nor resist.

#1568 DRIVEN TO DISTRACTION—Dixie Browning
An unofficial investigation led both Maggie Riley and Ben Hunter to sign up for a painting class. As artists, the advice columnist and ex-cop were complete failures, but as lovers they were *red-hot*. Soon the mystery they'd come to solve was taking a back seat to their unquenchable desires!

#1569 PRETENDING WITH THE PLAYBOY—Cathleen Galitz
Texas Cattleman's Club: The Stolen Baby
Outwardly charming, secretly cynical, Alexander Kent held no illusions about love. Then the former FBI agent was paired with prim and innocent Stephanie Firth on an undercover mission. Posing as a couple led to some heated moments. Too bad intense lovemaking wasn't enough to base forever on. Or was it?

#1570 PRIVATE INDISCRETIONS—Susan Crosby
Behind Closed Doors
Former bad boy Sam Remington returned to his hometown after fifteen years with only one thing in mind: Dana Sterling. The former golden girl turned U.S. Senator had been the stuff of fantasies for adolescent Sam…and still was. But when threats put Dana in danger, could Sam put his desires aside and save her?

#1571 A TEMPTING ENGAGEMENT—Bronwyn Jameson
He'd woken with a hangover—and a very naked nanny in his bed. Trouble was, single dad Mitch Goodwin couldn't remember what had happened the night before. And when Emily Warner left without a word, he *had* to lure her back. For his son's sake, of course. But keeping his hands off the innocently seductive Emily was harder than he imagined….

#1572 LIKE A HURRICANE—Roxanne St. Claire
Developer Quinn McGrath could always recognize a hot property. And sassy Nicole Whitaker was definitely that. Discovering that Nicole was blockading his business deal didn't faze him. They were adversaries in business—but it was pleasuring the voluptuous beauty that Quinn couldn't stop thinking about.

SDCN